A Town Like
No Other

A Town Like No Other

ELFREDA KNAUS

ISBN: 978-1-63821-067-2 (PB)
ISBN: 978-1-63821-068-9 (HB)
ISBN: 978-1-63821-066-5 (E-book)

Some characters and events in this book are fictitious and products of the author's imagination. Any similarity to real persons, living or dead, is coincidental and not intended by the author.

The Universal Breakthrough
42 Broadway 12th FL
New York, NY USA 10004

press@theuniversalbreakthrough.com
www.theuniversalbreakthrough.com

Printed in the United State of America

CONTENTS

DEDICATION

I would like to dedicate this book to my Daughters in Law
Michelle Knaus and Angie Knaus
I could not have done this without you.

Michelle spent many hours with all the paperwork
I am so grateful to her
She was always willing and patient, whenever I asked for help with
the manuscript
No matter how many times.

Angie came over many times, to help me with my old computer
(Which kept breaking down)
She came and fixed it, and was also very patient with me.

Most of all, I would like to thank my Lord Jesus Christ
I am forever grateful.

I personally had no idea what to write. He did not let me rest until
I sat down
And then the words started to flow
Whatever the Lord dictated to me, I wrote, until the book was finished.

So, I sincerely hope that this book will be of help to some people.

Elfreda Knaus

PROLOGUE

The Town in the Moonlight

The park was peaceful and quiet.

The moonlight filtered through the gumtrees.

It was long past midnight.

The park benches were empty except for one; way back at the end where the dried-up creek bed was.

A lonely figure of a young man was slumped on one end of a seat where it was darkest.
He gazed into the night, seeing nothing.

He was dressed in black leather pants, a jacket, and boots with shiny buckles.
The sleeves were cut out of the jacket, showing tanned strong muscles, covered in tattoos. His long dark curly hair was tied up into a ponytail.
A big hunting knife was tucked into his belt.
He looked very much like a young man, ready for a fight.

But he sat for hours without moving.

Then two young men, dressed in the same dominating manner and outfits came towards him.
Both laughed rather loudly and started to make fun of him.

"There you are, we looked everywhere for hours for you!"
"Turning soft, are we?"
"The big man has fallen? Huh?"
"Who is the boss now?"
Huh, Dan what's the matter... can't take it?"
Relentlessly they mocked him.

Soon, they got tired of the silent friend.

"You're no fun anymore!"

So they left, still laughing.

He did not hear a single word.
Death would be a blessing right now.
He never knew that a broken heart could hurt so very much.

CHAPTER 1

A Town Like No Other

When the storm settled, the people came out of their homes.

Slowly looking around, everyone realized that things were not the same as before.

Many of the houses were empty and the families were gone. But many had only some of their family members missing.

Deep into the night, cries were heard, but no one answered, or came.

Electricity was out and the telephone was also dead.
The little town was too isolated to get any help fast.
The next morning made things look a lot worse.

So the people gathered in the little market place to find out what on earth was going on.

Men started to argue, and nerves started to get raw, as to who should take charge. To find out what was going on, and why was this happening. What to do to fix this.

No one could find the police officer, or the mayor, who were brothers.

Both were considered to be overbearing Christians, and this did not go down well with some of the people. However, both men were looked up to, and the dealings with some hotheads in town always made the people feel secure. So, Jim and John, the two stable citizens had also vanished. Both families had gone also.

People became very angry, marching towards the little church, expecting the missing people to be hiding there. But as the door was flung open, finding the whole place empty, this made them speechless. No sign of the missing people.

Now what!

Sam the butcher took charge, he was very good at swearing and cursing and he let it rip.

The Pastor's house was next, this house was empty also.

Late into the night, the little hunting party went from house to house.

By sunrise, every house was visited by a now angry mob.

It was soon discovered that all the church-going Christians and all the children of the whole town had vanished into thin air.

Wailing, cursing, and screaming was the only thing anyone wanted to do.

Women were still calling out for their children.

Then word got around, that it was the Christians causing this and blame fell on them for this disaster.

The Christians said not so long ago, that Christ would come back soon and take them away. All had to repent and turn to Christ.

Sam the butcher and a few other men, wildly made plans to get even with God.

"Let's collect all the Bibles and all the books and destroy them."

With much enthusiasm and purpose, they went from home to home and ripped out all the books, even garden books, handyman books, and magazines, whatever was made of paper. The school had lots of books, so they took them all.

A giant pile was gathered by midday and the frenzy continued, destroying so much property, but no one stopped to think or be sensible in any way.

By evening it was worse.

Petrol cans were brought forth; cars lost the little petrol that was left in them, to feed the fire planned for the occasion, No one remembered that the petrol tanker was not due for a few more days.

The pub was relieved of its beer, wine, and spirits. A big party was planned.

As soon as darkness fell, the piled-up literature was drenched in petrol.

The explosion was gigantic, everyone cheered and everyone was drunk.

Soon the crowd began to fall asleep, right there amongst the empty bottles and dusty ashes.

The morning saw huge, burnt, black flakes dancing in the wind.

The golden sunrise was as if nothing had happened.

Another glorious day had begun…

CHAPTER 2

Tom's Nightmare

Tom walked around the house, from room to room in a daze.

Not knowing what to do or what to look for. Then his eyes fell upon Nellie's handbag, the one that she would use only for church. It was sitting on the side table by the front door, ready to go. It was, after all, a Sunday morning. He ripped the handbag open and pulled the bible out. It was in a cover and zipped up, bulging with a journal and stacks of notes and letters.

He carried it around the house, again from room to room, waving it over his head, talking rather loudly as if going crook on his family for not answering his frantic calls. His steps became faster and his voice louder. He acted as if someone was chasing him; Louder and angrier, round and round the house.

With one last effort and scream from the top of his voice, he flung the bible as hard as he could. With a big thud, it landed in the open fireplace. A huge cloud rose, then the dust settled down, the bible became part of the pile of burnt wood and ashes.

Then Tom fainted. He lay in the middle of his lounge room floor for a very long time. Then the evening came and the men from the village came to collect the books and magazines. Looking at Tom, some of them kicked into his side with boots and called him disgusting names. Then they left him where they found him and departed with all the literature that was so priceless to Tom's family, including all the photo albums, and the boxes and boxes of books.

Several days had gone by; Tom was still not seen much in town.

It was said, that some people committed suicide, many lost their minds. But no one cared one way or the other.

Sometime later, Tom was seen in town, wandering the streets at night. It was said that he was not right in his head, whoever saw him, kept away from him.

He never talked to anyone, never washed or shaved, just like so many others. His clothes became rags. He was avoided and yet he did not notice.

After the books, the next thing to collect was food.

Every house that was empty of people was stripped of its food. Electricity was still not working and the refrigerators had been left open and had a very bad smell.

Every shelf was emptied of food and tins, even dog and cat food started to taste delicious. Soon, even the dogs and cats were no longer seen.

No one said a word.

The mood in town shifted.

A small group became the dominant drive, bullying the weaker ones into subjection.

CHAPTER 3

Tom's New Life

Tom sat cross-legged on the kitchen floor, staring into nothing, just the way that he did for so long now.

A big flock of galahs landed in the old gum tree at the back of the house.

Suddenly, from the open kitchen window, the noisy racket of the birds entered Tom's ears.

He could hear again!

He realized where he was, and he sat right in front of the dog bowl. He could make out three dog biscuits, but why was green fluffy stuff covering them? He looked right at it and tried to work it out.

"How disgusting," he heard himself say, with surprise.

He called out his beloved dog Buddy, but Buddy did not come.

Slowly, he pulled himself up; his bones were so stiff and painful. Ever so carefully he looked around his home. Why was everything so strange? Why was everything so untidy and dirty?

The biggest shock came, when he came across a mirror. He stared at himself for a long time. He felt sick and tried hard to find answers.

His hair was long to his shoulders with a lot of grey on the sides. He never ever had a beard, but this one grew out of his own face and also had a lot of grey hair.

Hardly any food could be found in his kitchen, his stomach rumbled.

What on earth was going on here? Hours passed, but no answers could be found.

At last, he heard a soft knock at the back door, raising hope for answers.

Opening, he did not know this shabby old man. Was this stranger to be trusted?

"Who are you?"

It was Bill, a very old friend.

Bill stepped forward to greet his friend with a hug, but Tom looked suspiciously at him.

"Tom! It's me, Bill. I am so glad that you snapped out of it. I need a friend so badly; we have so much to talk about"

Bill looked as ragged as Tom, but Tom had to take it very slowly. It was all too much; he had to find a chair. He listened with a sick feeling of fear and unbelief.

Both sat for hours, a glass of water was all that could be found.

Again and again, Tom stopped Bill, to repeat what he just said. This was such an incredible story about all that had happened and had been going on in his hometown.

"This cannot be.... this cannot be true". Is all that repeatedly came out of Tom's mouth.

Then Tom understood why the whole house was so very dirty and messy. The bookshelves empty and the pantry bare.

Bill then explained to him, that with the disappearance of the people, some of the townsfolk concluded that it must be that Jesus took his people home and this scary talk was the beginning of the fear of the bible. So, the fire was the answer to them.

All of those missing went to church on Sundays together. Their wives, Nelly and Marg worked together, running the local nursing clinic.

Then, a few months ago, the church received a new pastor, who taught about everything the bible said; including water baptism by full immersion, and receiving the Holy Spirit with speaking in tongues, a new prayer language.

He explained, in following this, we become a born again Christian. Just as the bible stated.

This started to become a complication to some of the followers.

Bill was one of them, but so was Tom.

Marg told Bill, that living together was a sin and he would have to marry her or he would have to move out.

This made Bill very angry and he moved out.

Marg knew that Bill really loved her and she prayed for him and hoped that he would change his mind.

Instead, he had started drinking and became very bitter.

Bill continued, and then he took a deep breath.

"Straight after the storm had ended, and the people could not be found, the whole town went crazy. Anger was flaring and some bright spark started talking about burning the bibles.

The big bonfire and all the alcoholic drinks made it a bizarre night.

But the next day, I was in big trouble. I got the shock of my life. Nothing to drink!

I was so thirsty, I tell you, it nearly killed me. I then realized after some time of suffering, that I must be an alcoholic.

I so needed someone to hold me, I was so lost, I cried like a baby.

For a grown man to come to this state of realization is really a pitiful thing. Look at me now!

Then I had another shock. I so wished to be with Marg. Again I wanted to die, I really did.

If I had married Marg, like I should have, mind you, the fool that I am; none of this messy life would have happened to me and I would be with Marg, in heaven or wherever it is that she is.

But look at me now.

Pride, that's what it was, and I'm paying for it big time right now. Pride is a big sin I tell you."

Bill was in tears and Tom could find no words to comfort his friend.

They both sat in silence deep into the night. At dawn, Bill left to go home.

The next day, Bill came back, he had a lot of talking to do, and having a friend back from the dead was wonderful to him.

Tom was keen to hear some more, still marveling over the strange things going on.

A new plan was ready to be born.

As they talked, both remembered, that before the storm, that very Sunday morning, three buses were ready to be boarded, to go on special trips. One was a senior trip, going to Sydney for three days; the other two were for a school excursion. The planned trips were long in coming and everyone was so excited.

He pictured teary mothers and fathers waving the noisy kids off and others wishing the seniors a good trip and a happy homecoming.

So, both men marveled. What has happened to the buses? Did they all get back? Why is no one asking or talking about that?

Again silence, another mystery.

Why is no one fixing the electricity or the phone line?

Why is no traffic coming through town?

"This is getting spooky, it's like time is standing still. Aren't other people asking these questions?" Bill was whispering.

Tom had an idea. "Are you the only one that knows that I am ok?" Bill nodded.

"No one will bother you, as long as you keep to yourself; it's been like this for a long time now. No one cares. It's really sad."

"Good, let's keep it this way for now, till we work out what we could do. We have to try really hard. I want my life back." A determination was in Tom's voice.

"Oh, if we only could, I would do anything to get out of this nightmare." Bill's eyes went wet again.

"If it wasn't so funny, coming from me, I would like to say – let's pray about this."

They both looked at each other, surprised at this statement, and fell very silent again.

After some time had passed, Bill hesitated, but carefully asked, "Tom, why are you here? Can you tell me, why you are not with your family? I lost track of everything when I started drinking, I lost my normal life. You had such a beautiful life with your family and yet, you are here with me. Did something go wrong with you?"

Tom became very sad, when he looked at his friend, "Yes, something went very wrong with me. I have been thinking of nothing else since I woke up.

I rejected God and my family for many months. I discovered with great shock, that I am so very ashamed of myself. You know, everything starts so simple, and before you know it, you lose track of your senses. It was pornography. I spent all my spare time in those books and magazines, I could not put them down, I hid them in newspapers, pretending to read the paper. I spent for more and more. Thinking back, I just know that Nelly knew. She tried so hard to get me out of it, I did not see anything. I also remember now that she cried a lot and I was so mean to her. I called her names and was really nasty.

Funny thing, you know how I like reading books, and the stories of these magazines made me totally blind to the trap that I slid into. It totally consumed me to the point that I was not me anymore. This was an evil snare, I can see this so clearly now. How can a grown man be so tripped up? I am so ashamed of myself, but you know - when the town mob burned all those books, they did me a big favor actually. I lost my beautiful library; it took me so long to get it. I started as a child.

It's all gone up in smoke now! The price I paid, for being so very stubborn.

So much time to read, and there's nothing but empty shelves.

I did not want to go to church anymore, did not like my family, and said horrible things about everything and everyone. It must surely be my sin, what else could be so devastating.

Well, it looks to me, that we are both in the same messy boat. We have to see if we can find a way back to retrieve our lives, make up for it, get back on track, and do what we should have done in the first place. That is, if there is a way back."

CHAPTER 4

Planning a New Life

Next time Bill came back to Tom, after finding each other and talking things out - both had big hopes for a better future.

Where to start?

It was not easy to find a starting point in this hopeless place. Both men had business backgrounds, so a plan had to be made. This being a very private business and had very overwhelming frustration attached to it, as they quickly found out.

Tom, being a big reader had no books to rely on, not that he would find anything of this sort in any book. It was very frustrating to him.

"Ok, let's make a list of priorities, that's if we can find some paper and pen."

"What's positive around here has to come first."

"We are alive and not sick. That's a positive! I can't find any other points that would be any good."

Both looked at each other and became very depressed.

In the end, they had no food, raw nerves, and no plan. They were just very unhappy men. It looked so simple at the beginning, now they were shocked, to see a futile plan looking at them.

The reality was biting them hard.

"Let's try again tomorrow. Maybe we missed something important."

Bill went home and Tom wanted to be left alone.

He went outside, into the backyard, the sun was warm and he found a shady spot and sat down on one of the old wooden garden seats.

He closed his eyes. This was nice. The bees were humming and he desperately wanted to forget even for a little while.

He fell asleep and started to dream.

The voice of his Nelly cried out, "Buddy no, Buddy get down!"

That very same moment a big march fly stung him on the back of his left hand. With a cry of pain, he slapped the nasty fly with his right hand. His heart sank.

"Why did this have to happen right now? Can I never get out of this nightmare, not even for a moment?"

His mind went back to Nelly's voice. She must have some bother with Buddy, the two-year-old Border collie always getting into some mischief. Oh, how he loved that dog! He wiped a tear from his eyes and went back inside.

He noticed that lately, for some strange reason, he liked to sit in the middle of the floor in his lounge room. This shaggy little floor cover did not look so clean anymore, but it was soft and homely. He missed reading so much, with nothing to do but sit around, what is a person to do? "Is this my life now?" He said loudly to himself. "If only I had something to read! Even the Bible, the only book that I could not handle, even this one would be heavenly right now."

Time stood still. It hurt so much, having no control or say.

"What can I do?" It was a non-stop ringing in his ear.

He dozed off again and again dreamed of Nelly's voice. He was sitting in his chair, Nelly was on the phone, only half listening. He only wanted to know who she was talking to. He worked out that the other person was very upset because Nelly quoted some scriptures and said, "If you are truly sorry for your mistakes and ask God's forgiveness, but you must truly mean it from your heart, God will forgive you and set you free from all guilt and you will be happy again. I promise you that this is the truth."

Tom woke up with a start, her words still ringing in his ears. This was disturbing!

He remembered that day, it was some time ago, but he remembered.

Nelly belonged to a prayer group, she was always so busy with church, people are always asking for help and she loved to do it. He also remembered that it used to annoy him of late when she used to say, "Let's pray about this."

"Well now, let's pray about me and this nightmare," he said out loud. He startled himself, thinking this way, catching himself saying it out loud.

Then he realized that he was desperate enough to give in to these feelings.

"If only Nelly could pray for me right now, I don't even know how to pray for myself."

Desperation can soften the hardest man; he read this somewhere some time ago.

It seems to be true, he thought.

It kept at him, "Somebody has to pray for me; for Bill too."

Would Bill know how to pray? Would he?

Then he found himself seriously trying hard to remember something, anything at all. The Lord's Prayer came to mind. It was so long ago, he must have been a little boy, most likely. So he started to put his mind to it. He remembered ever so slowly at first… but the words did come and he found himself surprised at the joy that started to fill him.

Once the words started to flow, he did not want to stop.

This was amazing and wonderful, a feeling he never ever had before.

"Is this you Lord? Are you really here with me?"

Enjoying a new hope that filled his heart, he even started to laugh.

Then after some time of wondering and enjoying this lightness and hope, a miracle happened.

The way he was sitting, facing the fireplace, his eyes fell onto the pile of ashes. He had no idea why he wanted to stare at this dirty heap of ashes. It just felt good to do so. Some time passed and evening came. But looking at this fireplace brought so much peace, so he stayed right there on the spot.

Ever so slowly, without thinking, his eyes wandered all over the half-burnt wood, just browsing, till his eyes fell exactly onto the secret within. Amongst the round logs was something square, at first it meant nothing, but then with a big jolt, he sprang to his feet to retrieve this mysterious object. Wiping it between his hands, Nelly's Bible came forth. The excitement was almost too much for him. He cried and laughed, cleaning it some more. He unzipped the cover.

A journal and a big stack of letters fell out. The booklet was the first that he wanted to open. It was almost full and it was Nelly's handwriting. It was almost choking him, feeling so close to her. His fingers traced the writings and it was almost like touching her. But he felt that this must be private. He closed his eyes and took a deep breath, then closed the book again. "Oh, honey, I miss you so much," a whisper from the heart.

He leafed through the letters and put them down also. He concentrated on the Bible, and found so much of it had highlighted scriptures and underlines, so he started to read the marked ones first. When daylight came, he blew out the candle.

Lovingly he held the Bible to his chest with both arms, satisfied, and at last something good has happened.

CHAPTER 5

The Journey Goes On

The very next day, Bill walked into the house, "You look strange, what happened to you, you look funny."

So, Tom told Bill everything that happened since the time Bill went home the day before, leaving nothing out. From the insect bite, sticking his still swollen hand into Bill's face, to the time he tried to pray, and lastly finding the Bible in the ashes of the fireplace. He opened the Bible and showed Bill all the pages that had all the highlight markings in them. Tom was glowing with excitement. And to Tom's surprise, Bill became as excited as Tom was.

Then Bill remembered the present, wrapped in a not so clean tea towel, he handed Tom a little parcel. "What's this? It smells fantastic!"

"Oh, it's something I saved for you. No one knows that I got it for you."

He unwrapped the little bundle; it was a piece of roast meat.

He had not eaten meat for such a long time. It was delicious and Tom was very grateful.

They spent the rest of the day reading. Towards the evening, satisfied and relaxed, hunger lifted its ugly head and plagued them with a vengeance.

The subject came up about all sorts of things and goings-on in the town. People butchered all the animals around town, some even went out of town to shoot some kangaroo, but without a car, the hunters could not get close to them in the wide and open paddocks.

"What about the Harris farm?" Tom said hopefully, "It's a bit outside town, but we could walk."

"That's gone a long time ago; the Harris' would be devastated, if they could see what this beautiful place looks like now, I went out there a few weeks ago."

Both sat and reminisced over the delicious meals everyone had with this family. The Barbeques, the salads and smoked meat dishes, the lamb on the spit. The whole town was blessed with this lovely family.

Fritz and Rita came from somewhere near Munich, Germany, some years ago, they had two children, who now have their own families. The daughter lives in Brisbane and the son in Sydney.

Fritz and Rita bought this ten-acre very old farm about fifteen years ago. It was an empty and rundown place that no one wanted. Within a very short time, the land became the most beautiful garden. Old ways of farming, hard work, and lots of love went into it, and it all just bloomed. Everything just grew so well and all was shared with many friends. The place was really blessed with vegetables, meat, jams, pickles; the church was especially blessed with this loving couple.

To be told now, that this was no more, was unthinkable.

So they both decided to go out there and take a closer look at the old farm. The evening would be best. So they waited a bit longer.

Bill reminded Tom to walk the same way that people had seen him before. This surprised Tom. "What are you talking about?" So Bill explained that he walked a bit funny, sideways, and scratched his left ear all the time, never talked to anyone.

Both laughed and then found something better to talk about.

When the sun was setting, the two friends started off towards the farm.

It took only a short time before the farm came into view. It looked absolutely terrible. No mooing cows, no goats, sheep, geese, or chicken, and no flowers. This place used to be alive with noisy creatures and now it was dead and dusty from lack of water and care. It was all so very sad. Where was that big gander, which used to chase everyone? Or the shaggy dog that almost knocked him down every time he walked into the gate.

Oh, how he missed the cows and chickens and ducks, it was truly empty the way Bill had said.

Walking into the house, all the doors stood open, the dry leaves blowing in all directions in all the rooms. The kitchen cupboards had all the doors open and empty.

"What about the root cellar?" Tom wanted to know. Fritz always liked to talk about his pride and joy, his very own old fashioned root cellar. Walking outside and to the back of the house, the cellar door was still closed shut.

Did the thieves not know about this? The door was dusty, shabby, and uninviting. Excitement overtook the men. With much pushing the sticky door gave way with a great groan.

A cool breeze greeted them with the most wonderful smell of food.

Tom closed his eyes and said, "Thank you, Lord, you are so good to us!"

The shelves were full of jars with jams and preserved fruit. Big glass jars had some sort of watery liquid in them and filled with raw eggs. Hanging from the ceiling were big hooks with smoked meat and sausages. In one corner, there were large wooden barrels, with pickles and sauerkraut.

With pockets full of delights, it was much easier to go home to this miserable life.

Sitting till late into the night, bellies at last satisfied, the future and what to do was still a big question.

All answers are in the Bible, how can we find this one?

"We have to learn how to pray."

"Yes, we have to pray. The Lord surely has shown us that he is with us. Nothing else is left for us that is any good; it has to be the Lord." Bill agreed.

Praying and searching the pages in the dim candlelight had many rewards.

A new idea came together with so much peace and clarity.

"How many people are still around from our original group?" Bill thought a bit and then came up with some names.

"Let's see, there is the young couple, their twin girls had disappeared. Then the Gimmers, swallowed a stack of pills, they're gone, because their boys went. Can't think of anyone else at the moment; give me a bit of time."

"Do you really think that the rejection of the gospel truly left us all behind?"

Bill took a deep breath, "That's what it looks like to me, what else could be so devastating? That's why all the Bibles got burnt; somebody worked it out to be the truth."

"There is also an important bit to consider. If Sam and the others get wind of our plans and now the food, I don't want to alarm you, but it could be really dangerous for us. I don't trust them. You never know what they might be capable of. Something funny is going on with them; I can't put my finger on it, but every time I see them, cold sweat runs over my back. I can't make it out. If you ever see one of them, see if you notice anything. They are strange, odd. Something is very wrong."

Changing the subject to something more cheerful, Bill was ready to start a new mission. Very carefully, he would see if he could find any of the church people who would be trusted on a new venture and join them. He left in a very hopeful state of mind.

Tom went back to read.

Something new was about to happen, he could feel it. He had some more studying to do. What amazed him the most was the fact that he understood everything that he read, so clearly!

He became aware of a big need to share this new knowledge. He caught himself reading out loud to himself in a whisper, listening to himself. It was all so very exciting. At dawn, he decided to go for a walk. He felt so alive.

No one would be around at this time of day and he could think better in the coolness of the early morning.

The wind was a bit strong, making his hair fly in all directions. "How did my hair grow so long and so fast? And this beard is such a pain!"

But Bill was right, cutting it off now would draw attention, and they didn't need more trouble. It was not nice to discover more white than black hair on his head.

"Long hair at my age! And a beard and all; ha, what next?"

He shook his head.

Walking through the park, Tom noticed a figure of a young man sitting on a park bench, half-hidden in the shadows. He did not look right. Should he leave him alone or should he see if he needed help? Tom wondered.

Softly, he moved a little closer. But the young man was not responding. Tom put his hand onto the young man's shoulder; but again, no response.

Standing right in front of him, Tom noticed that no response at all was present - and no awareness at all, nothing. The only right thing to do was take him home. Pulling him to his feet, he led him like a blind man by the hand. Bill might know him. Taking him home was easy, he was totally incoherent. He would take no food or drink, so Tom took his clothes off and put him into bed in the spare room, covering him with a blanket, then he put his hands onto the young man's head and prayed for him. This act gave Tom a very new amazing feeling of being useful and so much peace. Praying for someone had a most wonderful reward.

The back door opened and Bill came in.

Bill saw the leather outfits on a chair and became most alarmed.

"Yes, we have a new house guest, do you perhaps know him?"

Softly, Tom opened the door to give Bill a look. But Bill almost had a fit. "That's one of Sam's boys. This is bad news. We have to get him out of here, this is Dan, he has a younger brother named, Jim, bad news Tom. What's the matter with him?" Bill was most upset.

But Tom had other ideas.

He reminded Bill of the time that he himself was so ill, that he did not even know who he was. This young man looked the very same way. "Bill, this feels so right, and I prayed for him. He is really very sick".

"You must remember these boys, Tom, think back a bit. Danny and Jimmy, their mother, Sue Penner, got into so much trouble with her husband because she took the boys to church with her. He is a sailor and away a lot. He made the boys swear to deny Christ before he went back to the sea. Now with no father around, Sam got hold of them."

So, Tom and Bill prayed some more, and then it was time to plan a church meeting.

CHAPTER 6

Let's Have Church

"Yes, we are on the right track, I was very careful and took it very slowly. Some of them were more than ready to talk about the Lord. Asking all the right questions, mainly, if there is any chance for them to be forgiven. Some of them even started to cry." Bill was getting very excited. This was really good news indeed.

Both sat deep into the night, planning a church meeting for the next evening. Inviting the more reliable ones first and taking it from there.

Tom was so keen; he wanted to find the right scriptures for the night, with the most important questions for the people to come straight from the Bible.

Bill arranged the seats and prepared some refreshments.

Both men were extremely nervous to do something so daring and completely out of the comfort zone for both of them. Again praying for the Lord to guide them, to do His will and have the boldness to speak.

"I found out that people are afraid of you, so give them a little time to get to know you. I am saying this because you might get some funny looks."

The evening did not come soon enough. Tom memorized most of the words, the candlelight was not very bright and he wanted to do everything just right.

"Nelly is not here, but I know the Lord is. Nelly would be so proud of me," he sighed.

As the people started to come, Bill showed them to a seat.

Tom had his hair neatly combed back and in a ponytail, it was the best he could do and he looked ok to them all.

Then, all wanted to know if forgiveness was really possible. Tom had many scriptures ready for them. He told them all why both he and Bill believed that it really was so.

They also talked about the finding of the Bible and the food and how God was in all this.

Then he proceeded to tell them about finding people who wanted to praise the Lord, the way it was written.

"It all points to one thing, can you see this? We have been given a chance to openly repent to God, and worship Him the way He wanted us to do in the first place.

Or, go back to the miserable life that we had, say, yesterday.

It's that simple."

All agreed. Promising to be careful and not speak to the wrong people for now. Sam and his mates would become very nasty and no one wanted that, but life would be a little bit better for all of them.

It was safer too.

God was making them safe and that's the most important thing of all. Every other evening, the church would get together after dark. Understanding the scriptures more and more, what a blessing it was, to open the Bible and learn from the heavenly Father.

CHAPTER 7

Closer to his Nelly

Tom's days were filled with reading. But some days he found himself holding Nelly's notebook and the stack of letters. He wished so much to ask permission to read all this, it looked so inviting. Telling Bill about it made him feel a bit guilty.

But his friend had other thoughts, "Look, Tom, we have a lot to learn, it might be that we have to let God guide us and these writings are really for us to learn even more.

Nelly would not have kept all this if it was not something important. The journal might be a bit more private, I would leave them alone if I were you, but the letters might be beneficial for us."

That sounded like good advice.

Did she pour her heart out in this journal, she did write a lot, he knew. So this one was out for now.

Thinking back again, he could see what a disgusting person he was.

"Nelly will never know how sorry I am, I must have hurt her so badly, I wonder if the Lord could tell her and that I am asking for her forgiveness and I am so truly sorry for hurting her so badly." He decided to talk to Bill a bit more on the subject.

He knew that he was not the only one with such heartache.

The letters might make him feel better. He picked the shorter ones first to see why she kept so many of them. Maybe something special is in them. Some looked old and fragile with the handwriting fading. Most were handwritten and some had been typed with the old typewriters. No one had these anymore.

Then one name caught his eye, it was a letter from Rita Harris! Why should she write a letter when the women saw each other almost every day?

Settling down once again to read, he would enjoy this one, he knew the person and that made it much more intriguing. Opening it, he could see that it was a written-out dream. This sounds interesting, he thought.

CHAPTER 8

The Letter from Mrs. Harris

Sometime in the year 2002, I had a lovely dream.

I visited several groups of people.

They did not see me at all. But what was so interesting to me was,

That every group of people I came across was a prayer meeting.

Intense praying was going on…

It caused me great pleasure and I was delighted with this wonderful sight.

My interest was especially sharpened by the different languages of these people.

It was not in tongues as all of them spoke some words in agreement.

Not all of them, but some of them were huddled together in a hidden dark room,

With a little dim candle in the middle of a bare table.

It all seemed to be very secretive, these people were obviously hiding.

And so it was, I popped up from one place to another, with great delight.

The prayers were so intent, that I longed to find out, what the subject of all this praying was.

Each set of people had a different language and therefore must have been in different countries.

Some of them sounded Russian, others Italian, some French and so many others that I could not place.

Then to my surprise, I ended up in a German group, this one I understood.

But how I knew that all of them prayed for the same thing, I cannot say.

In my heart, I knew that it was so and I was all ears…

"Let every soul find God."

"Let the Word of God go to all the people, who never heard the Word of God."

"Let the Word of God go to all mankind in all nations."

"Let the Love of God penetrate prisons of ignorance."

"Please Lord; soften the hearts of your people."

On and on it went.

It is my desire to join in and pray with them all.

Tom read the whole thing twice; he then folded it up again putting it back into its envelope.

He sat for some time before he picked up the next letter.

A soft knock at the back door told Tom that Bill had just come back.

"Are you ready for tonight? Have you been thinking of what we talked about?"

"Yes Bill, we will do what you suggested. I fully agree. Let's do it. And since it's your idea we will do it exactly the way you said. The Lord gave it to you and put it into your heart.

I think it's a brilliant thing to do."

Both knew this night would be emotionally taxing to all of them.

The people had been told that this night would be on the heavy side and all should be prepared. Those not ready or serious enough should stay home for this one night.

It would give others a chance to get things off their chest.

God willing, it will be as hoped.

So, Tom and Bill started praying for this night, asking the Lord to lead them in this quest.

Evening came and all was ready, looking nervously at each other and wondering if anyone at all would turn up.

Maybe no one understands the significance of what we are trying to do.

"It's in God's hands."

Time seemed to go very slowly.

Then came a soft knock at the back door and one by one, everyone arrived.

All of them came, thank you, Lord!

No one spoke. Everyone was very nervous, not knowing exactly what was going to happen this night. Every single person had a special request to put to the Lord this night.

Then Tom rose to the front and slowly said, "This is a very special day for us, Bill has offered to lead us in prayer and we will put our hearts into this very earnestly. We are of one mind in this. Bill wants to be the first one to do this. Every person can join in and have a say. Bill, it's all yours."

CHAPTER 9

Bill Opens his Heart

He came forward and stood, slowly looking at each face, clearing his throat, he started to speak…

"I believe I can speak for all of us here. The life we had before is gone, the life we now have is like hell on earth. There is nothing, absolutely nothing left for us.

Time is standing still so to speak. We are trapped in this. The only thing is the knowledge, that in our hearts we know that we blew it, big time!

Which is good; because we have learned that our connection with our God is still retrievable.

Otherwise, our God would not have put so many signs our way."

Closing his eyes, Bill started to pray, tears rolling down his cheeks.

"My precious Lord God, with a heavy heart I come to you to ask for forgiveness for my stupidity, blindness, and pride. I neglected your Word and ignored your ways.

There is nothing in my life that is any good, but the only good thing that I now can see is you.

You filled me with such a treasure in the past few days, now all I need is to ask for your forgiveness and to be with your people who are now my brothers and sisters.

I want to serve you and be some use to you in whatever way that pleases you."

With these words, Bill went down onto his knees and sobbed.

For some time all was very quiet.

Then, starting with Tom, one by one, they stood up and prayed in the same manner that Bill did. Overcome and remorseful, they all ended up on the floor.

Time went by and peace filled the room.

Being so still, it became clear to them that a very loud sobbing came from the bedroom next to them.

Tom remembered young Danny, opening the door, the young man was in the middle of the floor, sobbing his heart out. He wore the old jeans and tee shirt that Tom had laid out for him.

"That's the young man from the park." Tom explained.

"Danny, is that you?" Bill asked him, to make sure he had the right person.

Danny was very embarrassed. But with the goings-on of that evening, no one even noticed. Helping him to his feet, comforting him and a bit of food was well received. Then Danny started to tell of his life.

CHAPTER 10

Danny's Story

"Oh, my God! All of you, praying like you did - has set me free.
Thank you, Lord, thank you, all of you.

It seems that I just woke up from a dreadful nightmare. I found myself in this dark hole and I could not get out. Then I heard you praying and I started to listen with all of my might. Your prayers were like my very own words, from each of you."

One by one, the people started to remember the boy they all knew, commenting on the big difference his clothes had made on his appearance, and how all were scared of those young men, dressed in leather gear.

Then, later Danny recalled his life, sadness etched on his face.

"We had no way of knowing how far this was going to go."

He spoke slowly, concentrating and wondering, how all this was going to sound.

"Sam has a big influence on a lot of folk around here. We were depending a lot on him for things. Mainly food. But we started to run out of meat some time ago. This was the beginning of hell. We did not see it coming, at least I didn't. Sam has a friend, who drives a road train. This friend sometimes makes a short stop for a break, when he passes through in the middle of the night. This is when Sam buys a piece of buffalo from him. Sam was very convincing, the only problem that we could see, was that one of our young friends went with the truck driver. Never saying goodbye to us which had upset us. Sam thought that that was funny. But we believed him.

The older men, Sam's old mates had a very bad habit. Well, we called it a bad habit.

Every time a beast was slaughtered, these men would retrieve the blood and drank it, while it was still warm. The subject came up a few times, the older fellows together with Sam, started telling us younger ones about the butchers of the old countries who liked to drink the warm blood of the animals. They were very proud of those stories and other old tales."

Danny stopped and looked at the little group with so much sadness and heartbreak, that he was told to stop for a break.

Every one needed a break; and a pot of tea was a good idea.

It was getting late, but no one wanted to go home. Everyone wanted to know why Danny was so very upset.

"I think I have to get this off my chest once and for all, the reason for this dreadful nightmare."

Finishing the last drop of tea, he put the cup down, letting out a big sigh, he continued.

"The other day, I walked into Sam's backroom, Ron his mate was in front of me.

Ron brought the last bag of salt from the Harris farm in a wheelbarrow. So Sam did not see that I was there. But what I saw made me want to die."

Danny trembled and took a deep breath.

"My young brother was hanging upside down on a meat hook by his feet and Sam had a bowl, holding it under Jimmy's cutthroat. All went black around me. The next thing I know, I heard you all praying and now, here I am."

Everyone was speechless. Not knowing what to say or even believe what had been said. Is there an answer to anything like that? No one even ever heard of such a tale. The room went very silent.

With a trembling voice, Bill almost whispered, "Tom didn't I say the other day to you, that Sam and his men looked a bit odd to me? That's exactly what they look like. When I was a boy, my grandfather said exactly the same thing about drinking animal blood. Those men also became bigger and looked strange. Look at domestic cats that go wild, and feed on birds, the same thing, they also become bigger."

Then he added, "Animals always knew and feared those butchers."

This news was even worse, it confirmed Danny's story.

Then, one of the men asked Danny. "I really don't understand. Why aren't you and your brother with your mother? You always went to church and your mother was such a lovely lady, always going to church. But you boys did get left behind. What happened to you?"

Now all eyes went back to Danny, who explained about his father finding out, he did not believe in Jesus, did not believe in God. He called their mother bad names and forbade the boys to go with her. "He made us say words that denied Jesus and cut us from God, he was very cross with our mother and full of anger."

"Father was not home much, always at sea and we did not see him much."

"Then when you prayed earlier this evening, Jesus understood my dilemma and fully pardoned me, he took me back, but in my heart, I just know that he never really left me. But I don't know of what will come of my little brother, I so hope that he has been forgiven like me and that he now is with my mother. That would be so wonderful."

Bill put his hand on Danny's shoulder. "You were a child when you gave in to your dad, you had to, but now you are old enough to make up your own mind, your own decision and that counts now."

All agreed. It was very late now and slowly the moon changed after some more talk, most of them went home.

The rest stayed together till the morning. Danny would stay with Tom from now on.

And Danny was very grateful.

CHAPTER 11

A New Visitor

Dan was a good company. He was very private and kept to himself in his room a lot, only asking for something to read. Tom gave him one of the longer letters.

A very soft knock at the front door made Tom look up from his reading.

Who would this be, no one ever came in the day time, let alone the front door. It was agreed that this would be unsafe.

Quietly he went to the window to spy on the person, before deciding to act. It was a woman in her early thirties maybe. He never saw her before and for a moment could not decide what to do, pretend not to have heard her?

She knocked again, a little louder this time. She did look behind herself to see if anyone had seen her.

Tom was not sure but was interested in this mysterious person.

Opening the door just a little bit, he asked her why she was here.

"Please, can I talk to you for just a moment?"

Her voice was somewhat unsure as she whispered: "I made sure that I was not followed, but I would very much like to ask you something."

So Tom let her in and quickly closed the door behind her.

He led her into the living room and offered a seat.

She settled down and looked at him with a bit of fear in her eyes.

"My name is Joan Fletcher; I live with my husband two streets to the left from here. We moved to this town only a short time ago. The lady next door to me invited me to come to this house with some other ladies.

All the others were friends with your wife and they wanted to meet me. This is now some time ago and they all disappeared. I had such a great time and I needed to know so much of the things that they talked about, I never heard about Jesus the way they spoke. Now they are all gone and I feel so very lonely. Your wife had a letter that she read out to us, I was wondering if you knew about it and that you could tell me the story of it again. I can't forget about the little girl who talked to Jesus.

At the time, my husband was so very angry with me when I told him about my new friends, he will not talk about God in his house, he said. This was very upsetting to me; I had no idea that he felt this way about God. My husband Tony is now close friends with Sam, I don't like this man. With this darkness in this place, I just know that I had to come to see you. I don't know you, but it feels so right."

She stopped talking and fiddled with her hanky.

Then she added, "I can't recall the other women, can't find them. I don't know what to do, but I only remember this house. I feel like I am missing out on something very important. Coming to you is so strange, because you are here with the rest of us."

Then Tom knew why she was here.

He invited her to the next meeting with the strongest urge for secrecy, like the rest of them.

Before she left, she asked him again about this letter that Nelly read to them. Being very fragile and old would be a good clue. He said that he would try to find it. Tom also reassured her that all of them were praying for protection and he would put her name on the list with all the others to be saved and protected.

He sat in silence for a long time, contemplating this new situation. This again could only be from our God. He prayed, "Thank you Lord for gathering your people - even in this town. The danger is in this place for sure, but we trust you Lord and that's how it is."

But how long this will last was the big question.

He wanted to resume his reading but could not get back into the flow from this morning.

So he went back to the pile of notes, one was a very thick stack of typed papers.

That one would take a whole day to get through, it looks like a study of something, he thought.

Going through the letters again, Tom picked up a thick letter for the fifth time, addressed to his wife. This time he would read it.

So Tom settled down and started reading.

> *Dear Nelly,*
>
> *I thank my dear Lord for finding a friend like you. You have helped me so much.*
>
> *I needed someone to talk to and you came along. As you know, I found it very difficult, telling you about my experience with this dream I had. It was so hard to put into words. So, I want to apologize for taking so very long to answer your request, it was even harder to put it on paper than to speak about it.*
>
> *I cannot thank you enough for praying with me and getting this burden off my chest. I feel so much better about it all now. Because I have learned the underlying message of this dream.*
>
> *God bless you and your family. Love you, dear sister in the Lord.*
>
> *Annie.*

Here is my Dream.

In the year 1980, I had a very disturbing dream. At the time I was a newly born again Christian. Everything was very new to me. Before this time, I never had any disturbing dreams. I found it hard to understand why a loving God would allow something like this to happen to me.

Here is the dream or nightmare...

The whole world was in chaos. Fear and anger were rampant.

The movie Blob comes to mind. It was something like it, only much worse because I was right in the middle of it. The world news media, all television stations echoing the same dreadful disaster. These happenings were throughout the whole world.

I was petrified with fear, the same as the people all around me.

I could feel it, I could smell it, come to think of it, and I can still smell the fear of those days.

Mind you, it started quite funny. People laughed at it at first. It was first discovered in England, the size of a car. But it soon became a nightmare to discover its gigantic appetite for earthly things, fear started when it became apparent, that it grew in all directions. It grew in size so fast, that it started to scare even the military.

A most powerful and unusual fear started to grip all nations.

But absolutely nothing could stop it. All weapons of the entire military, all the machinery in the world were tried.

It absorbed bullets, even bombs. It took at all like a special treat. Samples needed to be taken to examine the thing, but no one could get near it as it sucked everything into itself. It rolled along, in every direction and so became a massive Blob. It looked like a very thick custard, but reddish-brown, sometimes like dead blood and shiny. The whole world was a delightful treat to this thing. It absorbed absolutely everything in its path.

Houses, skyscrapers, cars, trains, trees, animals, and people. Everything got rolled onto and then disappeared. It kept growing and no one could find out where it came from and what it was made of. It was easy to see that all the earth was tasty food for it.

Then England was gone. It was one giant big blob.

It was hoped that the oceans would stop it, but it loved to devour the big waters the same as the land.

One by one, the countries vanished. The news was now brought from airplanes only.

Australia was now the last place left. Many people had come from other lands, bringing personal horror stories with them. Overseas was now silent. The Australian Air Force went all over the earth to find survivors, but found none. Many planes that ran out of fuel on the way here just fell into that thing. All was gone!

Australia was surrounded by every side, right around…

The panic made people go crazy, and losing all hope was the main stress; without hope, people perish. That is so true.

Many stayed home to die with the family. Many took to the outback, in the middle of Australia. My family went with most of them to the outback.

With many cars and trucks on the road, it made it almost impossible to get anywhere.

Petrol became a big problem, it was soon exhausted and the food and water are the next dilemma.

What went on amongst all the people was not nice. Hate, fear, theft, and violence became an everyday thing.

Walkers were in the thousands in no time now, begging for food or water. It was a heartbreaking sight and so many lost children.

Many gave up, just sat down on the bare ground, hugging families and sobbing. It was all so very useless and everyone knew it. It was all just a matter of time now; the blobby enemy had been seen now in the distance. It was much higher than was expected. But the misery would soon be over.

"Let's get it over with," many cried out.

My family and I had left the car behind, like the rest, walking with the crowd, so very tired and so very thirsty.

People were dropping all around us from exhaustion. No tears left to shed. All around us, only dry dust and half-alive bodies.

I found myself among the last ones, only my oldest son was left with me, still by my side. He was a teenager in his prime. He always thought that he was bulletproof. But he was also so very tired. He turned around, to look at the thing coming towards him.

I looked at my son with so much pain in my heart. He let out an ear-piercing scream, raised his fists toward this death, and ran the last few steps, and then he was also gone. My family was no more.

I sank to my knees; I was also ready to die.

As my knees hit the ground, my mouth fell open, and little silver balls started to float out and towards the ugly blob.

The very first little ball that touched the target made the thing stop in its track and all the other silver balls hit the target, one after the other and the enemy started to reverse.

People that were still with me started to scream and scream and scream.

They came to me and picked me up off the ground, "How did you do this? What are you doing? Where did you get the shiny balls from?"

All of a sudden, the reversing of the blob made the entire previously swallowed up thing pop back out and back to the way it was before.

It came back the same way that it was taken. The land, the people, and the cars were all back.

My mouth was still pouring little silver balls.

Then I woke up… I was totally exhausted, then I heard my own voice, I was praying rather loudly speaking in tongues.

I felt very confused, very tired, and very safe.

This dream was so scary and lasted so very long. I was so very worn out and my eyes had been puffy from crying.

For days I could not sleep well. The images from that night kept coming back.

I turned to the Lord, to help me with this because it would not leave me alone.

But thanks to our Lord, he sent my dear friend to me and as we prayed, he gave us the answer.

We realized that I asked the Lord a question the night before that dream. I wanted to know, "Do I really have to speak in tongues?"

"How do I know that this is really from you?"

"Why is speaking in tongue so important?"

"What is it for?"

"What do I do with it?"

And my Lord showed me how, why, and what for! Thank you, Lord!

Still, after all these years, thinking about this, the fear that can beset people, especially the ones without God, is a frightening thought. He really looks after us. And thank you Lord for sending Nelly to me.

Tom reread the whole thing. What a good lesson, for all of us! The others will have to read this too. The importance of learning God's ways and doing things the way that he wants things done can't be stressed enough.

It's a matter of trust, obedience, and faith.

Picking up another letter, he wondered if this was the one that the young lady from this morning was referring to. It did look old and fragile, the handwriting was fading. Carefully he unfolded the paper; it actually was in three parts, with the last one not so old looking.

CHAPTER 12

Little Girl under the Kitchen Table

The First Letter:

The little girl under the kitchen table

The little girl sat under the kitchen table, peeping out from the shadows, trying very hard to be invisible. The screaming and yelling this time was about her. She wondered frantically, trying to find out as to what on earth could she have done so wrong.

A young man often visited this house, he always argued with everyone. With aunty and grandfather, it was always political, but grandmother was never even talking to him. He was never welcome in this place, always disturbing this peaceful little home.

The little girl feared this man.

He came one day when no one else was home and he screamed at the top of his voice with grandmother. This man always screamed. Most of the time the girl saw big red swirls surrounding him, as he got angrier the swirls got redder and it was this red color that was so frightening to her.

The girl had a secret friend that no one could see, so this last time this red appeared again she told her friend about this frightening red color and that it again upset her. From that moment on, the red color was never seen again, but the screaming continued.

Grandmother yelled back at him. "Take her, I don't need her, she is yours anyway."

To be given away to this man was too much for her, she froze.

Time stood still.

One day, a young lady, who often came to visit and brought lollies, often talked to the girl. She said to grandmother, "Has she said anything yet? Is she talking anything at all?"
"No, nothing."

But this time the little girl heard the conversation, she heard for the first time, how much time had passed, she had no way of knowing.

Grandmother had a lovely voice, as she was dusting and busy with housework.
She always sang. Being attracted to her voice, the little girl started to listen to her.
The songs were very old ballads. The funny part was that she sang harmony, all by herself. But it did sound good.

Then one day the words became understood. That was very bad news for her. The songs were about children, unwanted children. Tales told of children locked into closets, taken to the woods for the wolves, sold to gypsies, all of them unthinkable nightmares for children.
All this knowledge about giving unwanted children away or selling them played a big part in the mind of this small child.

But she was never alone, that she knew. Her little secret friend was always her. She also expected and waited for a special lady to come to her one day, who knew exactly what she needed and loved her exactly the way she was. She even had a picture of her in her mind. But she would spend the best part of her life, looking for this person. One day she would find her and bring her peace.

The Second Letter:

In my grandfather's garden

It is the month of May, spring time in Europe.

Again I am reminded of a time, long ago, and my childhood in my Grandfather's garden. The last Sunday in the month of May is a special feast day called the (Pfingst) Sunday. It is the day of Pentecost Sunday. A welcome holiday time even if you are not a catholic. The Pentecost roses are in full bloom and it is the middle of spring. I think these roses are called Peony; we had light pink ones and dark pink ones, lots of them. Beautiful perfume.

All the fruit trees were in full glorious blooming splendor and the garden had masses of flowers of all colors, with busy bees buzzing, colorful butterflies dancing in the sunshine. I just loved it there.

I was about 4 years old and I sat on the dusty ground, way back in my favorite corner of the garden.

The sky was a beautiful blue, the sun warm and high; a glorious day.

Behind me was a white painted wooden garden bench, which sat across the corner. The high lilac bushes and mock orange sat between the fence and the wooden seat.

I sat with my back to the bench and the corner. In front of me was a semicircle with the Pentecost rosebushes. To my left and right was the footpath and the rest of the garden had all the other flowers in all brilliant colors. All the flower beds were raised and sat a bit higher than the dusty ground that I was sitting in.

There I was, a little girl deep in thought and contemplating about the meaning of life.

Surrounded by irises, pansies, forget-me-nots, daisies, violets roses, the flowering fruit trees.

The bees, the butterflies, the golden sunshine, they all suddenly disappeared. The sun became rather dull. All at once, the brightness of a very strong light caught my attention. It came from the top of the Pentecost roses right in front of me.

At the very same time, a gigantic silvery dome formed several meters around and above me. A hushed quietness filled the space. Then a humming of strange music filled the round dome.

It was the flowers, singing and pouring perfume with their nodding heads!

I could see the stream of it flowing toward the now appearing figure of a tall, white, and sparkling form of a man, who was that bright light.

Exquisite perfume surrounded us! Bewildered and in awe, I looked back to the ground.

I knew who stood before me.

The flowers, still nodding towards Him, also knew who he was.

They were worshipping their God.

This was not of earth. I did not dare to look any closer, as he stood right in front of me.

His garment was white living light and it moved as he moved.

My heart and my soul screamed as one, "My Lord, My God."

Over and over again.

The hem of his garment was all that I dared to look at, it was shimmering, it was alive.

Then He sent a ball of light right into my chest and entered my heart, it was the most beautiful and warm feeling to experience.

It caused me to hear him as he spoke, giving me a clear understanding and I spoke the same way to Him.

Many things have now come to pass, but I wished that I could recall more of it.

We could talk, it was speech, without the spoken word, but I heard and spoke in my heart.

"Your family will love me the way you do."

"This day you have been set free from family curses."

"One day you will write a book."

Now this one really scared me all my life. He never told me what I was to write about. I still don't know.

Love, so overwhelming was poured out all over me, everything was so alive.

Then I started to rise, lifting and floating upwards with such lightness, off the ground. I felt so very tall, then I found myself standing behind Him, it was then that I noticed so many other people in long white robes standing behind Him with me. I wore the same white gown.

So much love was being poured out from all of them towards me. It showed that they all knew me. I cannot recall knowing any of them.

We stood about one and a half meters above the garden on solid ground.

I looked down and saw the little girl sitting on the ground in the dust, looking up, but not moving.

The feeling of belonging to these heavenly beings was so overwhelmingly right, so perfect and so completely peaceful.

As we stood there, three little girls, only one of them was older than myself, came towards me. One of them was my younger sister Trudy, getting closer, something alarmed them and they started to run towards me.

As we looked down on these approaching children, something happened on the inside of me and my heart was filled with a strong desire and compassion, all sorts of knowledge rose up within me, concerning human nature.

This new feeling drew me back into my little body; I can still recall a little shiver.

Just in time as the girls grabbed me, held me, hands all over me, testing my body, a little fearful and excited at the same time and shouting at me, "What was this? What is this?
What are you doing? What happened to you?" and so on.

I had just said that I was fine and all was ok.
But I do know that I felt that I was glowing.
I did smell the perfume and felt the waves of love for a very long time.

I had written this into a notebook a long time ago.

Then one day, I was writing about something entirely different, when I had a sudden flashback of this day.

I recalled clearly, that prior to sitting down on the ground, I was in a very depressed state.

As it was my habit in those tender years, I talked a lot with my secret friend, a little boy named Jesus, who was about the same age that I was.

He was there, any time I needed Him. I told Him that I did not want to live in this world anymore, because people are too hateful and nasty, always screaming at each other and I could not live in a world such as this.

Jesus gave me an entirely new outlook on life; it did make me cope and still does.
I can still feel the love and the smell of perfume in my prayers.
But from that day on, the little boy Jesus became the Christ who loved me.

The last letter:

(This one did not look so old, but seemed to be part of it.)

I found her

When I was in my fifties, I had a dream that really surprised me.

I dreamed that I stood in my grandmother's kitchen.
(My grandmother had passed away some years before.)

I went to the kitchen table and bent down to look under the table.

The little girl sat there, waiting for me.

It was the strangest feeling, I went down to her and scooped her into my arms and held her so close to me.

She put her arms around me so tight and we both cried.

We sat this way for a long time, and then I woke up.

It was a very fulfilling moment for me.

One empty spot in my heart was at last at peace and she will always be there.

—⟋⟍—

Tom sat for some time, thinking.

His own childhood was so very different. His grandparents had lived in a cattle station in the Northern Territory. It was always so hot there. Almost every school holiday was spent there with his two brothers; riding horses, chasing cattle, swimming in the muddy creek, and getting into all sorts of mischief. He had a wonderful childhood. Growing up with all the things that boys really loved to do.

Later, his grandfather bought trail bikes and we boys got to ride them as well. It was heaven on earth and my brothers and I had the greatest time riding them.

One of the farmhands, old Jess, no one knew how old he really was, or so we had been told, showed us how to trap rabbits and catch fish in the creek or get rid of a snake, that had gotten under a bed in the shearers quarters. Everything was exciting in those days.

But, how times change! A different lifestyle takes over.

Then Tom remembered where he was and the time that he could not escape no matter how hard he tried.

Trapped in a nightmare! He compared this present life with the one he had a few months before, and then back to his childhood.

What on earth is going on with me?

Becoming angry, he caught himself in time before Bill entered the room. This is no good, getting upset; we are in the same boat. Everyone was looking for something positive in life to hang onto and so far, all was going well with them.

But remembering his childhood again did give him such a jolt. Pulling himself up, fighting tears and trying to smile was a big task at this moment.

Depressing as it was, it had to be overcome, for others, if not for himself.

"Bill, you have to read this one, it gets a bit heavy at times but it's worth it."

"Any way, what have you been up to? Is there anything new in town?"

"No, but I did get a funny look from Sam, they did a bit of whispering behind my back.

His mates are shifty and big gossipers. I do hope that they aren't getting any ideas about us. That would be a disaster for us, now that we are getting somewhere good."

Bill took the letter and went outside into the backyard to find a shady spot.

Tom remembered the young woman; this could be the letter she referred to. It sounds so much like the one.

It is very interesting, Tom thought.

Danny knocked, with the last letter in hand and asked for more to borrow. He handed him a green envelope, it had a Christmas sticker on it and said that it had two stories in it.

Danny left with a grin. "I think Danny boy likes these stories too," Tom mused.

Then he went through the stack of letters again and found one that looked Christmas like. So he decided to read this one.

CHAPTER 13

My Special Christmas Eve

My childhood had a very special meaningful Christmastime, as long as we could spend it at our grandparents' house. The first few were the best, as I lived with them. It was all so very secretive. In Europe, it is still this way in many families. The European weather at Christmas is always very cold. The snow can at times be up to two meters high and also very frosty.

Cold weather like this has no perfume at all, so when the time came for Christmas baking, you can smell the biscuits from every house that you walk past. It always made your mouth water with sheer delight.

And so it was, also at my grandmother's house. It was all so hush, hush, adding to a child's imagination.

A day or two before the big event, the door to the main room got locked. Whispers and giggling and big smiles among the grown-ups. Then on the big day, all the family gathered for the main meal, it was always fish, potatoes, and salad.

Then my grandfather was the one to watch. He would get so very excited at this time! After the meal, he disappeared into the locked room.

Then, when he came out, with a big shout and ringing a little bell as loud as he could, he ran through the hallway toward us!

"Quick, quick, the Christkindl is here!"

We all ran around the corner of the hallway and stood at the open door. Big eyes, mouth wide open, and out of breath - the best moment in a child's life had arrived.

It's Christmas Eve!

In the far corner were the Christmas tree, dozens of flickering candles and sparklers, shiny balls, chocolates, and sweets hanging on the tree. The pine tree had a wonderful fragrance that filled the room. Around the tree, the floor was covered with gift boxes in colorful paper. In the middle of it all, a very beautiful nativity scene, that was as old as my grandfather.

As all the family stood around the tree, we all sang:

"Silent night, Holy night"

It was very moving.

At that very moment, my Lord gave me a very special Christmas present.

For the length of the singing, the room had no walls, and round about us, many, many angels were singing with us. Also, the light around us was not from the candles on the tree, but the brightness came from above us.

It was a very Holy moment for me.

When the singing ended, all went back as before, it left me disappointed.

It would have been wonderful to have more time to contemplate on the vision.

But the noise of the ripping of paper and happy shouts made it impossible.

It was time to get stuck into the biscuits and lollies that smelled so good for so many days past.

But this Christmas is the one that I will have forever in my heart.

Bill had arrived and seeing Tom busy, he went to Danny's room. The two were becoming good friends, and it pleased Tom to no end, it felt like family.

So he picked up another letter. This one was in a pretty pink...

CHAPTER 14

The Very First Time I Met Jesus

Later in life, I read scriptures, saying how important it was to be as a little child.

I was in my cot, ready for the night. My grandmother was tucking me in, "Time for your bedtime prayer," she said.

"Little boy Jesus come to me,
Make a good child out of me,
My heart is small, but room for you only
My precious little Jesus boy, Amen."

As I repeated my grandmother's words, I understood every word that I spoke to Jesus with all my heart, soul, and mind. I totally opened my heart to him. I had no reason to think otherwise.

As I gave my heart to Him, I felt His presence with a wonderful glow of warmth and peace. It was just wonderful, as I gave my heart to Jesus.

But I also knew at the very same time that other people did not believe the way that I did, so I kept it a secret to myself, all through my childhood, I talked with Him and He with me.

He visited me every time that I wanted to talk to Him.
I started to see Him, a little boy about my age.
I never told anyone as I felt that it had to stay clean.
He was my secret friend.

The world is so very polluted. I longed to stay a little child that was clean.

Being part of the human race, with people so nasty all about, it became harder to stay clean.
I felt like being spat on and spewed on by other people.

Then I met God the Father

On very hot summer days, the storm clouds brought the thunderstorms, with lightning and thunder. This was never a welcome visitor for me. At times like this, I was always glad when my grandfather was home.

He would walk up and down in the kitchen with his hands in his pocket; now and then he would stop, look towards the ceiling, and nod knowingly. I was frozen with terror from all that lightning and thunder. But my eyes were fixed on his face, wondering, what can be so funny at a time like this. Now I know - that he did this, because he knew that I was watching him - but then I did not get it.

When an especially heavy thunder cracked into the air, he turned to me and said:

"You know what's going on, don't you?"

I violently shook my head, all ears. With a big grin on his face, he pointed towards heaven. "Oh, our heavenly father is playing ten pin bowls with Peter and John and all the other apostles. Wow! Another strike!"

That was news to me, grandfather was amused. I was not.

But then I understood something...whatever God the Father does, cannot hurt me. Besides, He was, after all, the Daddy of my dearest friend, Jesus, who knew all about me.

This seemed simple to a child.

Opening another letter, Tom settled himself in a shady spot in the garden.

CHAPTER 15

1985: Heaven's Gates

I walked along, following the crowd. I felt like a zombie, so very dead to anything and everything around me. I could see where I was, could feel the cool floor under my bare feet, but why could I not think or respond? There was nothing wrong with my eyes, I could feel and see where I was, but why was I on automatic?

I could not snap out of it. Everyone around me was so happy, but my feet moved on their own along with everyone else.

I saw the greatest gate, wide open. Throngs of people. Thousands of them streaming into this fantastic hall. The splendor of this place was breathtaking and enormous, the ceiling too high to see. Apart from my eyes and feet, nothing in my body responded. From a sort of a distance, I could hear a lot of noise and goings-on; the people were in awe.

All the people were barefoot, and all were wearing white gowns and were so very happy. There were laughter and praises of joy and awe. But I could not respond or care about anything, was I dead? I also wore a white gown.

The throngs kept coming, through the great door, mouths open, heads turning. Every age, every race, young and old. All looked so very healthy except for me.

Barefoot strangers, streaming in, more and more still coming. In awe of all the splendor human eyes had never seen before.

The ceiling is so high, the floor is like golden glass, and the size of this room seemed to be endless. The air was also strange, a total absence from dust, a clean that was absolutely alive.

Ushers were busy, sorting through the people, in long white robes, looking truly elegant. People of all nations and ages had to be sorted into different groups. These heavenly servants seemed to know every single person by sight. And still, new arrivals kept streaming in.

I just kept walking, my feet moved along. I was aware that I did not care, but saw everything. People got sorted out around me, I just stood there.

One usher walked up to me and said, "Will you follow me please?" So I did.

Her voice was so gentle and kind.

We walked through other great halls and massive rooms. There were lots of people sitting and standing and talking. They were all so very happy to be there.

I was still in a frozen state of mind.

At last, we came to a smaller room that was made of glass.

I looked into the room, it had no end that I could see, and it went on and on.

In it, it had rows and rows of beds, these rows of beds also had no end.

In these beds laid very still patients, covered very neatly with brilliant white sheets, faces pale and eyes closed.

The dead in Christ shall rise first, "Is this that room? I don't know."

The room that I was in was a little elevated from the great room before me, as I looked down, I saw a group of people in brilliant white robes, standing in circle, several men and women in deep conversation. The usher turned to me and whispered to me gently, "Wait here please." I saw her go down to the group and heard her say, "She is here," bowed down and left. One man lifted his head and looked straight at me.

That very moment that he did, my life jumped straight back into me.

I immediately knew who was looking at me.

He came into the room, opening His arms with a big smile; I let out a loud scream and flung my arms around His neck.

His face kept changing from my father to my husband and to my sons and to Jesus in between them all. It was kind of weird. Then His face remained. I cried and wept all my sorrows and pain right out, till the tears became tears of joy and then I laughed with Him.

Waves and waves of pure love covered me. His peace filled my whole being.

More waves of love.

I was summoned to heaven, for my broken spirit to be healed.

This is what my Lord did for me.

For many years, I felt that I was at the edge of losing my mind. It was a very frightening time. Something within me would quiver and vibrate and I could not make it stop. It was like a cobweb at the point of breaking.

This had always been a big fear to me, that one day I would not be able to respond to the world around me. Being able to hear and see everything, but paralyzed to respond.

This is the stuff, my nightmares were made of.

This went on for many years.

I pleaded and prayed for my Lord to help me. Then one day, He did and I am very grateful.

CHAPTER 16

Notes to Remember

Then Tom found some loose notes... It said:

Notes to remember!

Without the soul, the body is a vegetable.
The soul comes from God.
It is given with love but it belongs to Him,
To be taken back, whenever He wishes.
To disregard a loving God is not only foolish,
But also dangerous to our very existence.
All belongs to Him.
He is the creator of all and He loves His creation.
He wants to talk to His people in all they do,
He wants to be part of His people's lives.

Honor Him - Praise Him - Please Him- Worship Him.

These people are my bride and I love her, if you love me, you have to love her.
Until you love her, my bride, you cannot love Me.

For these people that find it irritating to hear about God and Jesus, the Creator, the Bible, etc. Ever wondered why?
Chances are, it's the truth that irritates them.

Are you strong enough to face some facts of life, before you hit the dead-end of your road? To stand before Him, by the way, which you will, naked and with a red face. Don't take that risk, because you will be so very sorry in the end.

God loves His people.
While we fight with people, argue, lie, swear, hate, and generally disagree,
We unknowingly dishonor God.

Truth has no value if fantasy, arrogance, and pride rule.
Forgiveness is an act of the will; refuse to hold on to any unclean attitude.
To live without truth means to walk towards a dead-end.
You are surrounded by my goodness. Goodness before you, goodness behind you. Look for my unfailing love as it overruns the world and spills into every corner.
In sweetness and in sorrow, I am good to you.
In life and in death, I am good to you.
Think about all my all-surrounding goodness.
Psalm-25:8, psalm 33-5, psalm 34:8.

I am glad that you are my God. I'm also glad that you said, "Rejoice in your tribulations."
I don't understand this.
But you are my God, my tribulations are big to me, you alone know that all this might be for something good to me. I am so glad that I am in your hands.
Tribulations or joy, If I should fall, you are there to help me up.
If I get lost, you know where to find me.
If I should die, you will come and take me home.
I am all yours.
No matter how hard we try, we will always struggle to stay on top of things.
No sooner have we mastered one obstacle, two will take their place.
The answer to it is written in our manual for life; the Bible.
It's a marathon to the sweet end.

Life is nothing but a puff of air, but what you and your soul learn together, will live forever. The directions and choices of learning make a difference.

If you think you can make it on your own because you think you know it all, have all the answers, and feel great about yourself,
Think again, in one split second, your life can be the opposite.

Life is like an original recipe. The moment you change one little thing ever so slightly, it is not original anymore.
In God's plan, we are not supposed to get sick, be unhappy, or even die.
But man, in his puffed-up head and great wisdom changed things, sometimes a little, sometimes a lot, and with it the Word, that God penned carefully for man's own good.
Now all mankind is stuck with the result. Until we go back individually to Him, to ask for forgiveness and get back to the original plan.

Life is like a supermarket, you can stay as long as you like, look, handle, and pretend to buy. But in the end, you will have to go home, which means you have to go through the checkout and pay. As we will at the end of our life, only one way out.

CHAPTER 17

The Armor of God's Soldiers

The very next morning, picking up the pages of the typed notes, he settled down to see what it was. The heading sounded interesting.

Finding a reference stuck to the front page, Tom suddenly remembered something very exciting.

This was about the new book, which had just arrived before he went to Sydney. It came by post for the family library. He intended to read it as soon as Nelly was done with it. Come to think of it, that's when he started to slip so badly.

With new enthusiasm, he settled down to see what Nelly found so interesting.

The book was called "Dressed to Kill" by Rick Renner.

Tom remembered the book well; it was on a hardcover, a very nice looking book.

The title was a bit, well, unlike a book Nelly would read, but she was so taken by it and she made so many notes. It must be special.

Taking the Bible onto his lap, he first wanted to see what the scriptures would say about the subject…

The Whole Armor of God:

Ephesians 6:10-18.

10 Finally, my brethren, be strong in the Lord, and His might

11 put on the whole armor of God, that you might be able to stand against the wiles of the devil.

12 For we wrestle not against flesh and blood, but principalities, against the rulers of darkness of this world, against spiritual wickedness in high places.

13 Wherefore take unto you the whole armor of God, that ye may be able to withstand in the evil day, having done all, to stand.

14 Stand therefore, having your loins girt about with truth, and having on the breastplate of righteousness.

15 And your feet shod with the preparation of the gospel of peace.

16 Above all, taking the shield of faith, wherewith ye shall be able to quench all the fiery darts of the wicked.

17 And take the helmet of salvation, and the sword of the spirit, which is The Word of God.

18 Praying always with all prayer and supplication in the spirit, and watching thereunto with all perseverance all saints.

So Tom settled down to read Nelly's study of the many pages in front of him...

The Whole Armor of God.

Ephesians 6:10–18

Sturdy Belt of Truth. Breastplate of Righteousness. Shoes of Peace.
Shield of Faith.
Helmet of Salvation.
The Sword of the Spirit. There is also a Lance.
Put on the whole Armor of God.
The full Armor is to defend and protect - primary one's Mind.
This is my responsibility - to be a sharp Soldier in full Armor.
To stand tall, head high, shoulders straight, ready at all times.

So, stand guard until the job is done and the battle is won.

For this is for your life and your fellow soldiers, family, and friends.

Stand firm, stand guard over your mind, which is the battlefield Satan uses to destroy lives.

Finances, Businesses, Marriages, Emotions, Health, your Body.

He will use other people to do so.

A sober decision, a walk by faith, a way of life.

We are equipped to beat the daylights out of foes.

God has given us... Three Offensive Weapons, Three Defensive Weapons... And One Neutral Weapon.

The breastplate, the shield, and the helmet are <u>defensive weapons</u>.

They protect, give confidence and assurance to move forward in your spiritual growth.

The <u>offensive weapons</u> are the shoes, the sword, and the lance. Weapons that enable you to enforce and demonstrate Satan's already secured defeat.

The <u>neutral weapon </u>is the belt of truth, which is the Word of God. It is the central piece of spiritual armor, the written Word, the other pieces of armor cannot function properly in your life without it.

All these weapons come from God. You must draw your spiritual weaponry from God.

Since Paul was surrounded by this huge military machine and bound to a heavily armed Roman soldier; it was, therefore, logical that his thoughts would turn towards the issue of spiritual warfare and spiritual armor.

The environment was perfect for the Holy Spirit to begin speaking to Paul in such terms. There at Paul's side was a perfectly dressed and fully armed soldier who had been trained in the skills of warfare.

This soldier was literally — <u>Dressed To Kill</u>.

At the time, the Roman army was an advanced military machine; it was the world headquarters of the highly developed — Roman Army.

Paul was chained to one of these soldiers.

With this formidable image constantly at his side day and night, Paul began to receive exceptional spiritual insight into the Holy Spirit regarding our own spiritual weapons.

He recorded this revelation for us in Ephesians 6:10-18.

About ten years earlier, Paul wrote in the epistle Thessalonians about spiritual weapons. 1 Thessalonians 5-8.

Day after day, week after week, year after year, Paul was side by side with a heavily dressed, trained killer.

Through his time of roman imprisonment, Paul had become closely acquainted with the nature of the Roman soldier, who was a killer of the worst order.

Murder and violence were ingrained in these men and had become a very integral part of their nature.

Now Paul uses this very graphic, dangerous, and murderous example to show us what the spiritual weapons that God gives us can do to a spiritual foe.

God has provided us with His supernatural power so we can effectively use the Weapons of our warfare to contend with unseen, demonic powers.

If you are mentally prepared and alert to know how the enemy operates.

You have already eliminated potential attack, you have won the battle.

The Belt of Truth.

God has not left us naked before the enemy.

Your belt seems to be an insignificant little thing until you take it off.

Your pants might fall down, you become untucked and you can look a mess. The belt holds things together.

The roman soldier's belt had the shield; with a clip in place to hold the important and protective shield.

There is only one spiritual weapon that is visible to sight.

The belt of truth — it is the word of God.

When you put on the belt of the Word and determine to make it a priority in your life, you are well on your way to winning your battle in life.

When you ignore the Word of God and cease to apply it to your life on a daily basis, you have willfully chosen to let your entire spiritual life come apart at the seams. You will come undone.

For Christians who neglect the Word of God, it is only a matter of time before they feel condemned in nearly every area of their lives.

Let the Word of God stay with you.

As we give our minds to the Word of God, the Word itself begins to build a measure of deliverance, safety, preservation, soundness of mind, and healing into our lives on every level.

Never forget: The written Word of God supports everything else in your walk With God.

You need people around you who understand the centrality of the Word as much as you do.

The teaching of the Word from the pulpit should only confirm what you have already heard God say to you through His Word during the week.

It is important to note that the Roman soldier was completely covered by his armor. Every single piece had its own place and importance.

He wore it with pride and was constantly testing his skills daily with other soldiers.

The Breastplate of Righteousness.

Ephesians 6:14. Stand therefore, having your loins girt about with truth, and having on the breastplate of righteousness.

Righteousness is a weapon - it is the breastplate.

How can this be a weapon?

The soldier's breastplate was extremely elaborate and beautiful. Made of bronze or brass, usually brass, very shiny, a dazzling spectacle.

Righteousness can make you shine, it is not only a defensive weapon to protect you from the blows of the enemy, but it is also offensive to assist you, assaulting the enemy and taking back lost territory.

Because the devil desires to penetrate and immobilize a person's mind and emotions; he especially delights in finding believers who do not know that they are righteous. They are easy prey. No word of condemnation, no false allegations, no guilty thoughts will penetrate your heart or lodge in your mind when you are walking in your breastplate of righteousness.

Your mental attitude has everything to do with how well you perform in the midst of a battle.

When a believer finally grabs hold of the truth that God has graciously imparted Righteousness to him, it will change him.

An attitude of righteousness will profoundly affect your prayer life. You will step out boldly to do the work of God.

When you walk in righteousness, you wear a weapon of defense against the enemy's slanderous accusations and insidious strategies.

With your breastplate of righteousness fixed firmly in place, God's glory Radiates from your life to all those around you.

Shoes of Peace.

And your feet shod with the preparation of the gospel of peace.
Ephesians 6-15.

Peace not only protects you, but it also provides you with a brutal weapon to wield against the enemy when he attacks — under your feet— a firm footing.

A solid foundation positioned firmly in place, without fear or intimidation.

A peace that prevails; a conquering force, a supernatural peace.

Before you shift blame for a personal failure to someone else, take a moment to examine yourself, see if you left a door or even a little hole open somewhere along the way that gives rise to your current dilemma.

Before you run out to fight the devil off your back, look in the mirror, the devil is not always the source of your problem.

Peace gives us a foundation so secure that we can step out in confident faith without being moved by what we see or hear.

When you are walking in the peace of God, you often don't realize how difficult your predicament is.

This supernatural peace pulls all the plugs on the devil's effectiveness. If he can't disturb your peace, he can't disturb you.

Bind peace around your emotions the same way the Roman soldier had to bind his mostly brass shoes, which were in two pieces and tube-like with spikes. These shoes were exceptionally dangerous to a foe.

Let the peace of God call the shots in your life. Let the peace of God referee your emotions and your decisions. Let the peace of God umpire your life and your actions.

With the peace of God operating in your life, you can walk through the roughest, most difficult situations and never get bruised, or seriously injured.

Satan's only rightful position is under your feet, completely subdued.

The Shield of Faith

The next piece of Spiritual Armor.

Above all, taking the shield of faith, wherewith ye shall be able to quench all the fiery darts of the Wicked. Ephesians 6-16.

It is imperative once again to point out that the shield and the belt were inseparably linked to each other. The massive shield of the Roman soldier rested on a small clip attached to his belt when not in use.

The lion belt is the representative of the Word of God—the Bible—your faith is attached to the Word of God, you will always have the dependable, ever-present Word—the lion (loin?) belt of truth to build your life upon and to give you direction. It is always on hand. It is the only weapon that you can see and hold.

All other weapons are spiritual and invisible to the eye.

A Roman soldier had two shields, one was small and pretty for parades, with past deeds inscribed, and the other was for battle in war confrontations. It was heavy with six layers of leather. It was large and he could cover himself fully from his enemy.

The Holy Spirit selected this second shield. He is telling us that our faith makes certain we are completely covered, just like the soldier.

He had a daily duty to do to his shield. He had to oil it daily, or it would start to crack and break. He also had to soak it in water, because the enemy used fiery arrows. All had to be perfect for all types of battle.

Play it safe and assume that your faith always needs a fresh anointing to keep your faith alive, active, and well.

We must make certain that we allow the Holy Spirit to freshly anoint our lives with oil on a daily basis and saturate our faith with the water of the Word.

Faith is designed to be out in front where it can completely cover you in every situation of life.

It is impossible to overemphasize the necessity of a life of faith.

When a believer puts away his faith, it always leads to a spiritual shipwreck!

The Helmet of Salvation

In Ephesians 6-17. And take the Helmet of salvation…

The Roman soldier's helmet was a fascinating and beautiful part of his armor. Flamboyant and intricate, with engravings and etchings, a huge plume of brightly colored feathers or horse hair straight up out of the top of his helmet. The helmet was made of bronze, right down to his cheeks and jaws. It was extremely heavy.

It had to be strong, to protect him from hammer and battle-ax.

This helmet undoubtedly made a soldier noticeable.

So, why would the Holy Spirit compare a weapon like this to salvation?

When a person is confident of his salvation, and walking in that reality, that person is noticeable!

To face the adversary without your helmet of salvation is the equivalent of spiritual suicide; a soldier's head would roll…

By exposing your unprotected mind to the devils lying insinuations, you are in a position to be deceived.

The mind is the control center of your life. The helmet is to protect it. Wear it snug and tight. Any little crack can be an opening for the enemy to take advantage of our emotions, health, family, and finances.

Comprehension of salvation and all it encompasses must be ingrained in your mind. That knowledge is a protective helmet.

"Put on the whole armor of God that ye may be able to stand against the wiles of the devil." Ephesians 6-11.

Wiles, devices, deceptions. How successfully can he deceive a believer?

The devil has used that same road for thousands of year, because it worked so well for him all the time. He plays mind games, but we are not ignorant of his devices. Corinthians 2-11.

When a strong knowledge of your salvation is wrapped around your mind, you will never fall prey to his deceptive tactics.

Deception becomes a stronghold, a prison.

The helmet of salvation becomes your freedom in your God and your walk with Him. Be what He has planned for you to be…

The Sword of the Spirit

Spiritual battles are just the same as natural battles.

God has given us spiritual weaponry so that when battles do come, we will be prepared to maintain our stance, and be in a victorious position.

The roman soldier had five different kinds of swords.

The first was the gladius sword. It was extremely heavy, and broad, with a very long blade, sharp only on one side.

The second sword was shorter and narrower, 17 inches long, 2 1/2 inches wide; it was a more popular sword, as it was easier to swing and carry.

The third sword was even shorter; it looked more like a dagger but was still a sword.

The fourth sword the Roman soldier used was a long slender sword, similar to modern fencing. It was not good for combat or battle.

The fifth sword was the type of sword that the apostle Paul had in mind when he wrote about the sword of the spirit; which is the Word of God.

This brutal weapon of murder was approximately 19 inches long. Both sides of the blade were razor sharp; making this sword much more dangerous than the other four. In addition, the tip of the sword was turned upwards, causing the point of the blade to be extremely sharp and deadly.

This one was a terror to the imagination; this one was a sword not only to kill, but to completely rip an enemy's insides to shreds.

This is the sword of the Spirit; A Rhema.

Thus, a Rhema is a specific word or message that the Holy Spirit quickens in our heart and mind at a specific time and purpose.

Rhema words are given and supernaturally empowered by the Holy Spirit to enable you to withstand the adversary's spiritual, mental, emotional, and physical attacks.

It is not necessary for a person to know the entire Bible in order to have the sword of the spirit/Rhema at his disposal.

Once received into the heart, the Word immediately begins working in those areas of the mind, which are off base and wrong.

The belt held the shield with a clip on one side and the sword on the other side. The gladius sword, being so heavy, had to be swung with both hands.

The two-edged sword in Greek writings is called the Distomus; di means two, and stomus means mouth. So it is the two mouthed sword.

In Revelation 1: 16 we read: "And out of His mouth went a sharp sword."

One sharpened edge of this sword came into being when the Word of God initially proceeded from the mouth of God.

The second edge of the sword is added when the Word of God proceeds out of our mouth.

This is the reason the original text calls the Word of God—A Two-Edged Sword.

The two-edged sword came out of Jesus first. That is why the Word of God is so powerful. It carries His Word out of the mouth of the believer.

The last piece of weaponry Paul lists in Ephesians 6:18.

The Lance of Prayer and Supplication

The word lance is not in Ephesians chapter 6:18, but the whole armor is to be used and the Roman soldier had seven pieces of weaponry. Ephesians 6 tells us the most powerful and necessary piece of all, without which any believer can live.

"Praying always with all prayer and supplication in the Spirit, and watch thereunto with all perseverance and supplication for all saints."

It tells us to put on the Whole Armor of God
We have various kinds of Lances,
We have various kinds of prayer,
When you Wield the Lance of prayer and supplication
This powerful prayer tool is thrust forward into the spirit realm against the malevolent work of the adversary.
Most Roman soldiers carried both a short and a long lance.

They had to be ready for all sorts of battle—and so do we…
We have unseen spirits continually seeking to bombard the flesh and hassle the mind of believers.

The basic types of prayer are found in the New Testament:
Prayer of Consecration
Prayer of Petition
Prayer of Authority and Faith
Prayer of Thanksgiving
Prayer of Supplication
Prayer of Intercession

We should never stop short of thanking God in advance for hearing our prayer.

The prayer of Petition is therefore a Prayer that exposes a person's insufficiency and his need for God. When we allow the Word of God to permanently and habitually lodge in our heart, that Word so transforms our minds that when we pray, we do so in accordance with God's will. The true intercessory ministry of the Holy Spirit occurs when you are at a loss for words; and don't know how to pray.

Suddenly and supernaturally, the Holy Spirit falls into place and joins with your rhythm of prayer.
Until we admit our utter need for His work in us, the Holy Spirit is limited in His ability to move freely in our lives.
No matter what challenge you encounter, your ultimate victory depends on whether or not you use the spiritual weapons God has provided for you.
God's desire is that you move forward boldly and courageously in prayer in order to seize His Will for your life and bring it into manifestation.

Prayer should always bring us face to face with God in an intimate relationship.

CHAPTER 18

The Mood is Changing

Tom was on his last page, when the noise of the two, Bill and Dan, made him look-up.

Laughter was a really rare thing these days, they both talked at the same time, excited about some of the letters and exchanging opinions on them.

He had to smile, this is so good, it really felt good, he thought.

He put his head back down; his own reading was also very good. It covered so many sides to so many questions. "I wished that I could get hold of that book, it must be powerful reading." But he knew it went up in smoke!

After some time had passed, the mood changed.

Bill and Dan called out Tom to come quickly to the window.

So he hurried, not exactly pleased to be disturbed.

He could not believe what he saw.

Five men were about to come into his front gate. Two carried rocks and two others, cricket bats. Sam was in the middle with his hands in tight fists.

Then the yelling started, "Come out you cowards! We need to talk! Open that…door!" Abusive words and threats, warnings, and promises were hurled towards the front door.

After some minutes the first rock hit the front door with a big crash.

Riled up and angry, the five walked up and down the front of the house.

After some time, with lots of threats, and colorful language, they left with the promise to be back soon.

With a sigh of relief, the three, although in shock, stepped back from the window.

"What are we going to do? This is going to get very ugly."

"We can't fight them, we can't talk to them."

"What a mess!"

So it was, being caught with a situation that has no good ending. But it became clear very quickly, that being scared out of one's wits would not give them any help or answers. Some time had passed with no solutions becoming apparent.

"We need to pray, that's the only thing we can do. We should have done this right from the start." But the mind was not in control, fear was.

"That's it," Tom said, "Lord God, we need your help!"

"Our God does not need fancy words, we are simple, and we need God's help, not his approval for our skill for words. So, just let's ask Him for His help."

Again full of hope, they prayed for help.

The day came to an end and so did peace. The mob that came was much bigger.

Now there were more voices, more yelling, more threats. Sticks and rocks started to fly, clubs waved.

"That's what I was afraid of for some time now," Bill whispered.

The crashes of rocks towards the front door were ear piercing.

Then one very big rock came through the window and hit Tom on the head.

He went down like a dead man.

CHAPTER 19

Wake Up Tom!

With a big sigh. Nelly placed the phone down.

Then she put the kettle on and got the teacups ready. She was very tired from crying all night and badly needed a shoulder to cry on.

The knock at the door brought a little smile back to her face. Opening quickly, she hugged her friends. Pastor Robert and his wife Helen both looked concerned at Nelly.

They settled down and Nelly took a big sip from her cup as if to draw strength from it. "You said to me if I needed help or if I can't cope to let you know, but this is not about coping. It's about something entirely different. Tom is still in a coma, as was expected, I was told. For some time now, I thought that he was waking up, he is mumbling in his sleep. You both remember how he stopped coming to church and the fuss he caused about the water baptism. He was very verbal about it and made no secret about how he felt."

Nelly stopped for a moment, took another sip from her tea and Helen reached out and patted Nelly's shoulder, wondering what was so mysterious and upsetting to their friend.

Nelly went on, "I can't understand what to make of this, Tom is speaking very clear at the moment, you see, he is reading the Bible."

Robert interrupted, almost in a whisper, "But Tom never reads the scriptures, he never had a Bible that I know of, are you sure, you heard right?"

"That's why I need you to help me. Every evening at the same time, he starts to read. Yesterday he was the clearest, he read the whole of Mark chapter 16, I usually sit with him at this time to pray and read myself, so I quickly found Mark 16 and read with him, I tell you, I still can't stop shaking."

"Would you ask your babysitter to come over, so you can both come and sit with me and see for yourself? I really have no idea, what will happen, but I am going nuts here. The kids have no idea as yet; they are both so very good and helpful. I need to understand what is going on. That's why I am asking you both to see what you think."

Robert shook his head and Helen gave Nelly another hug, the three sat silent for some moments.

"OK," Robert began, "Let's not jump to any conclusions, maybe it's something simple and we can figure it out. Mind you, I never heard of anything like this before, wow…"

"We have to be here a bit before six, we should be here and settled in his room and this will give us time to be ready without disturbing him. If he really reads the scriptures, that is not an ordinary happening. No, I never heard of anything like this before," shaking his head again.

The three had another cup of tea and some small talk. Nelly also told them that she had to get Marge's help the other day. The dog got in and in his usual excited ways, Buddy jumped right on top of Tom into the bed, ripping the cannula right out of Tom's arm, dislodging the catheter, and losing his head bandage. Tom started bleeding again and his restlessness spread blood all over the bed.

It took both women some time to slow him down and straighten the mess.

From then on, Buddy was not allowed into Tom's room, which had become a hospital room to take care of him for now.

After some more hugs, Pastor Robert and Helen left with the promise to be here at the appointed time.

Nelly went straight to the phone to inform Marg of all this and be here with the others. Then the evening meal had to be made for the children and herself. She asked them to be good; their father would have some visitors later this evening.

Nelly had her hands full with this very restless patient, it was so important to keep him still but he was anything but. So many times she thought that he was waking up, disappointing her every time.

Everyone arrived on time. All were very nervous. Pastor Robert suggested that all would pray silently and put everything into the Lord's hands.

It seemed a long wait. At times it looked like something was about to happen, but he became rather quiet.

After what was an endless time to the little prayer group, Tom took a deep, big breath and said, "This is a very important moment for us all, and since the Lord spoke to Bill about this, it is Bill's wish to go first. We must repent and let our Lord cleanse us. After Bill has had his say, others can join in and say whatever is on your heart. So, let's pray and Bill, it's all yours."

Everyone was dumbfounded and looked at Marg, who started to cry.

"This is Tom? Our Tom? The one who would not do this in real life? And Bill, is this our Bill, Tom was referring to?"

Pastor Robert shook his head again.

Bill was also at odds with the church.

My, my, what are we supposed to do with this?

All sat quietly again and made no attempt to say anymore.

One by one, they started to pray in tongues, what else is there to do?

Time went by and we all ended up in the kitchen for a cup of tea. The tea tasted good, but no one spoke a word.

"Should we try again tomorrow?" Marg said very hesitantly.

Helen raised her voice in a whisper, "This would be fun, if it wasn't so spooky!"

"We have to let this play itself out, nothing makes any sense right now, we do have to know what is going on and now he mentions Bill! This is getting very interesting!

Please let's not be frightened about this, we must trust the Lord, he must be doing something fantastic with us. Marg, is Bill still keeping to himself?"

Everyone looked at Marg, who nodded and became rather teary.

"Robert is right, this could be something very special, come to think of it, our daughter Kathy said something that I thought strange the other day, she was spending time in her father's room and was reciting the Lord's prayer, she said that Tom was repeating most of the words. I dismissed it at the time."

Then, Nelly shrugged her shoulders, looking from one to the other. It was getting late and time to call it a day.

"We will talk some more tomorrow. We wish we didn't have to leave you alone like this, it does not seem right. Tom will be back to his old self in no time and we can forget all this stuff. All will be back the way it was before." Helen sighed.

Everyone agreed, wishing Nelly a refreshing sleep and a peaceful night, then she was left alone, pondering her future.

She sat for a long time in the lounge room in her favorite recliner. Her arms holding her knees close to her chest. The words, Tom will be back to his old self in no time were ringing in her ears. Oh, no, no, I don't want his old self back!

It's too painful! No one knew how hard her life had been in the last few months.

She used all her energy in prayer to have Tom back the way he was before he left the church. Something dreadful had happened to her beloved Tom.

The time he went to Sydney was the starting point, she was sure of that much.

The business meeting took three days; he came back after five days, a complete and total stranger.

He brought her a present, but was totally shocked, because he thought that she did not like it.

Nelly could not get her head around this; never in all her life did she ever see anything like it. Black lacy underwear and black fishnet stockings.

It felt like it was made from wire and he fully expected her to wear it for him that very night.

She shuddered, just thinking about it.

From then on, he would not come into the bedroom; he was so very disappointed in her.

He no longer listened to reason, what type of woman did he expect her to be?

From then on they lived in different worlds. A very painful way to live.

Early, the next morning, the phone rang. It was Dr. Forbs, enquiring about Tom's progress. Nothing new was to be reported that Nelly could see, but Dr. Forbs was very encouraging and made her feel better. The news that Tom almost woke up and talks a lot was good news to the Doctor.

"He must be almost conscious, keep up the good work." Then he hung up.

Nelly was thoughtful, as she straightened his sheets. How will she respond to him, when he looks at her for the first time?

He was so very lucky, he could have been killed. Tom would not come with her when she took the children to the bus terminal. He was so very angry when he went for a walk. Anger was the only thing that she could see in his face, these last few months. Praying was her only comfort, secretly hoping that no one would notice, especially the children. But for how long?

Only Buddy went with him, a good thing that he did, no one would have known where to look for him.

When the dog came home in a frenzy by himself, Nelly knew right off that something was wrong. She quickly called some friends together for help. The dog was very brave and led them straight to Tom, who was pinned under the big tree, a fair way outside of town.

It was not that windy, but the tree was very big and very old.

A favorite spot for so many townsfolk, the trunk had so many initials carved into it, everyone was sorry about Tom, but they were even more upset about the tree.

"My Lord, what will I do, if he still rejects me? I think, we had a good marriage before, in my heart, I still want the same life that we had before, please Lord, help me."

Nelly's mind kept going in circles. Her heart aching for her mate to put his arms around her and give her comfort the way it used to be.

She looked into his room, Tom was looking peaceful, so she picked up a tall glass of iced soft drink and went outside to sit in the shade to quieten her mind.

But her mind did not want to be still.

She found herself thinking back to her childhood, thankful that her mother would never find out, how heartbroken she was right now. Or, would mother know what she should do right now?

Well, that I will never know.

Our children, Gary and Kathy, are both such good kids, doing so well in school. Their father has no time at the moment for them. Work is very demanding right now, he tells them.

Nelly wished that this was all that it was.

Her thoughts went back to Kathy, she was exactly the same age right now that Nelly herself was, when her mother sat her down and told her of her life at the same age of nine years.

"Kathy, you do not realize what a beautiful life you have, I will have to tell you the story of your grandmother at the age of nine…" she said.

CHAPTER 20

Mother's Story

Thoughtfully, Nelly recalled her mother's story...

The year was 1945.

The winter snow had gone, but the ground was still too cold for any spring greenery. The frost was still very heavy in the mornings. The people in the old home town were about to face a dreadful future, getting worse day by day.

Word was getting around that all able-bodied old men and schoolboys over the age of ten had to report to the council chambers at once.

The town had no other men left; all had been called up for service.

It was said, that trenches had to be dug round about the town and the now retreating armies would soon have need of them.

We lived about 15 km. north of Vienna and ours was the side of the soviet direction. I still remember seeing the heads of the diggers bobbing up and down with soil flying in all directions. And hearing the cursing of the old men, because the ground was still hard and frozen as they worked the trenches.

This was not far from my home, only three houses to my right.

Everyone was frantic. A date had been given as to when all this was going to come to pass. War was approaching our little town and

I still remember that we had only a few days to go and all of us were very frightened.

When the schoolchildren were told not to come to school anymore, that was a separate warning to us of the real danger. Even the children, that did not like school, did not like this at all.

Just before the worst took place, however, my mother came home from shopping one morning and in a great hurry, she explained to us all that had to be done right this very moment. All young women and children had to be evacuated from this town and it had to be today. We had to be at the railway station at a given time. My grandparents urged us on and pleaded with us to hurry and go quickly. The deadline was fast approaching.

But my aunty, mum's sister Louise, did not want to go; she had a little boy, Karli, who was my only cousin.

Her husband, uncle Karl, a soldier, was at the Russian front far away.

His very last letter was very disturbing to us all. In it, he wrote that he was in a field hospital with a bullet wound in one leg and that he could hear the thunder of the approaching enemy (Russian) artillery. It was common knowledge that Russians never took prisoners and that all hospitals were doused in petrol and burned. We never heard from him again. It was all very upsetting.

Mum spread a couple of blankets onto the bed and threw whatever onto it. She had not much time to think. Then she handed me and my two sisters all our clothes, "Here, put all this on!" "What all of this?" "Yes all of it!"

We giggled in a nervous sort of way, getting fatter by the minute; we'd never worn 5 undies and all the other bits before all at the same time. We wriggled around to make them, sort of, fit. But it was scary, that's why we must have giggled.

You only had to rotate the things once in a while, and no bags, that must have been the idea and it worked, it also kept us warm.

Then it was time to go and we realized that we might never see our home and loved ones again and this did hurt. But the faces of our grandparents were the hardest to witness. I will never forget the sadness of the moment.

At the railway station, all was ready. As we got onto the train, my father was there. He heard of our plight and came as quickly as he could.

His job was not a nice one; he belonged to a rescue team in Vienna that had to dig the people out of the bombed houses. A very upsetting task.

He brought a huge box of cracker biscuits with him, saying how sorry he was, that he had no time to find something better.

In parting, he said, "No matter where they take you, I will find you."

And the train pulled out of the station.

Our whole carriage lived on these biscuits; the box was almost a cubic meter large.

That's all we had.

The train stopped at no stations, it just kept going. We entered the higher country; the snow was still in some places. The many layers of underwear and jumpers kept us from freezing, a little bit anyway. There was no heating and most of the windows were boarded up. My dad picked us the only window with glass in it before we got to the train. That was a Godsend. So, most of the people crowded around us into our space, to look out the window. That also kept us warm, I think.

The children were very noisy, many babies crying all the time. The women might have known the country we were traveling in, I never thought to ask my mum about it, I think she knew, after all, Austria is a small country. As long as it was far enough from the front line.

We often heard warplanes fly over us; it did break the boredom a bit. But one day, the planes went right over us, turned, and came back to us; the train slowed down and then stopped. Just then the bombers went very slowly over us, as we saw to our horror that our train driver ran past us in the opposite direction.

It was all like in slow motion.

Then the planes were gone and so was our driver. Never to be seen again.

We just sat there for a long time, not knowing what to do. Some people started to panic, which set the children off. It was becoming unbearable. I don't know how long we sat there; after all, it was our only shelter. Some of them must have known where we were, because they left in droves, all fleeing in different directions.

In the end, we also picked up our bundles and started walking.

Small towns were found and packed with people like us. Young German soldiers also started to walk around, lost and begging for old clothes to get out of the uniforms.

Everywhere you looked, it was chaos.

It looked to us that the war was over.

One day, as I was wandering in a small town, a loudspeaker in the marketplace announced that Hitler was going to address the German people.

His voice was strong and clear like always. Everyone stood still.

"German men, German women…" he spoke for a few minutes, I can't remember or did not understand what he said, but that's the last time I heard his voice.

We lived in barns, in many barns, could not stay long in any of them, moved about a lot. But the hay barns were always soft and warm. Somehow dad found us and he and mum worked on a plan to get back home, as soon as it would be safe.

So many people are lost and confused everywhere. German soldiers moved about in droves, frantic to find a way back home. The Austrian soldiers had it a lot easier, they were in the homeland, it's all just a bit of walking distance.

But I will never forget the fear in faces, most of them just boys. So afraid to get shot by the roaming enemy forces, who, being victors, just for fun, were being very trigger happy. It was dangerous for some time, but it did settle after a while.

Big army trucks started to move in a convoy in all directions. My dad found some that went the direction towards Vienna, which was for us.

The danger of people getting shot was subsiding. The armies of the Soviets, English, and American became more stable towards the civilians.

We climbed aboard this huge German army truck that had just enough room for us, but it was a very tight squeeze. But at last, we moved towards home.

It was noisy, smelly, and oh, so slow. Yelling and cursing right through the cold night with very few toilet stops. Every nerve frayed, exhausted, hungry, and so very tired from lack of sleep.

Civilians and soldiers of all ages and nationalities milling around by the hundreds and the trucks could not move most of the time. The narrow country roads filled with travelers.

One morning, leaving the high country with its cold snow, word got around that in the valley, just before us, springtime had arrived. All was beautiful and green. As we drove down the mountain, we could hardly wait.

The tarpaulin was quickly rolled back and everyone was excited. As we came down the last hill, there was no more snow; it was so green with wildflowers and so beautiful. The road had large trees on both sides with the treetops coming together over the top of us. It was so green, lush with sweet perfume, and full of bees.

I felt that I was in heaven, on top of that truck I was so close to the branches. I really love big trees.

In my heart, I started to praise my Lord for his beautiful creation. I was in my own favorite world.

But ghastly outcries from the people around me jerked me back into reality.

So I looked down the ground to see disgust and horror. All of a sudden, the shiny sun went dark in my beautiful world.

"Where is God now? What is God doing about this?" On and on People lamented.

My heart broke at the sight. All around, on both sides of this road, this beautiful green valley was full of still burning vehicles of all kinds, tractors, cars, trucks, buggies. People milling around them. But the worst was the many dead horses. Big beautiful horses. With legs in the air in cramped-up position, mouths and eyes wide open.

No dead human bodies, I was glad about that. Someone must have removed them, I thought.

Such a beautiful beginning of this day with a nightmare ending.

We soon reached the parting of ways with the trucks and German soldiers.

Again we found a friendly farmer and moved into his barn, planning the next step to our journey.

A lot of horses roamed around, which the armies had to let go.

So my father rounded some of them up, to pick the gentler ones out, handy for our transport.

As he and mum herded some of them into an enclosure, one spooky one kicked my mum so hard that she went down and had to be carried out of the yard. It was a scary moment for us all. But she was very lucky; she got away with a very big black bruise on her back. She could not walk for some time.

With more care, we picked two very gentle horses out.

But what he picked was a great joke and a laugh to all who saw us!

One was a beautiful black mare, her tail went almost to the ground and her mane was also very long, we called her Lotti. A perfect horse for pulling a wagon.

The other one was also a mare, but she was most elegant. A very tall chestnut, long-legged with a black short bushy tail, and a short-cropped sticking up main. We called her Gretl. Everyone could see that she was not a workhorse.

Both horses became very friendly with us and we loved them.

A wagon had already been found which was in good condition and had all the necessary gear. We found a big tarp and hoops for us to sit under.

This was getting exciting for us; we really looked and felt like the American pioneers going west. The farmer gave us hay for us to sit on and also to feed the horses. We collected our few belongings and hopped on board.

My dad had found two young soldiers, who were farm boys, also looking for a way to get back home. Both were grateful to find the safety of a family and us, to find a way to learn to look after and work the horses.

Both the horses looked very beautiful and healthy, but hitched together, side by side, this looked nothing but hilarious. They looked silly and everyone laughed as we drove past. People pointed and grinned. But they did look like a funny pair. Poor Lotti, she did have to work very hard, but I must say Gretl did her very best.

But of course, my father had a very good reason for all this. He had a plan to get us safely back home. He heard of others, finding ways to get back home; after all, this was the only way to get anywhere. In the woods and forests, robbers waited and stole the matching horses off them and left the people stranded in the middle of nowhere. So, this was the only way to get through the dangerous dark forest. And it worked!

The armies, sometimes Americans, but mostly Russians had roadblocks every 5 or so km. Controls had to be made. What they were looking for, no one knew, but it made them feel important. The young men with us quickly went into the back under the blankets every time, and every time this happened, they turned as white as ghosts. My dad also did show signs of trembling and fear.

The stories that were going around in every town that we passed through were all very much the same. It added and fed the fear.

There was murder, rape, theft, and beatings.

Soon we had to part with one of the young men, and then the other, as we traveled through their districts. It was sad for us, but so exciting for them.

Somewhere on this road was my ninth birthday, we lost track of days and dates altogether.

Early one morning, my dad got very upset. In the middle of the night, the horses chewed the shaft halfway through, just at the point where the horses had to be hitched to it. No one knew how to get a new one, the town was very small. Nothing of the right size was to be found.

With great care, we went back onto the road, but much slower than usual. But suddenly, we got to a very steep descent down a hill, my dad could not get off quickly enough to hold them back and the horses took off. It all happened so fast and we were in big trouble. The chewed up timber shaft started to bend this way and then that. Then to our horror, we started to swing to and fro from side to side. It was getting hairier by the moment. Every time it looked like it was the last time, all the way down the hill. Then we hit the dirt, hard.

We landed on the grassy side, which was good; it was high, lush grass. The horses stopped right away and stood still, which was also good.

But the shaft was broken off, right where the horses chewed it.

The rest of us were not so lucky. The wagon landed on its side and everyone flew out, except for me, I was right under all our belonging in the grass.

Frantically, my parents dug me out. I never forget the fright on their faces, convinced, that I would at least have both legs broken.

This is how it looked to them at the moment. Love filled my heart for them. After some effort, I was finally free. With great rejoicing, I was manhandled to see that all my bones were ok.

And all was well, apart from the shaft.

So, the wagon had to be up-righted, which was no small task with two people and three small girls. But we were stuck with this broken item.

No farm or town in sight.

But just as we walked around in the grass to collect all our lost things, right on the spot that we had crashed into...

Was the exact item that caused the whole drama in the first place, a brand new one at that! We were speechless for some time.

Coincidence?

No comment!

"Thank you, Lord!"

It took us the rest of the day to exchange and replace everything.

But all was well again.

We sold Gretl for food and hay. I had this very sick feeling that she got butchered as soon as we left that town. Food was so very short in all places.

The last bit of our road, Home was very close. Lottie had only a very short way to go.

From our town was a little village, Dad knew a farmer that we called into.

The farmer was delighted to see us, he was a friend of my grandfather, knew my dad as a little boy. He was so happy to take Lotti, loved her and said that it would be the first horse in town again, and gave us a trolley for our things and some food. Only 2 km walking and we would be home.

The farmer had Lottie for many years; my dad visited her many times.

We walked the last 2 km. Our grandparents and all the others were so happy to see us, commenting on how well we looked.

We did not get our house back; the Russian army had moved in and made a bakery out of it. The big beautiful walnut tree in the backyard was only a black charcoal skeleton; I don't know how they did that.

We had more than twice the number of Soviet soldiers in town than town people. It was very crowded. We lived with my grandparents on my mother's side for many years.

The war had taken its toll on all the people.

My grandparents and all of them looked like skeletons from lack of food and living in fear.

No dogs or cats to be seen anywhere, money to buy food. There was none.

My grandfather Josef came to us one evening, handed my mother a bag, and said, "Here is some food for the kids, it's a roof rabbit," and he left, saying that he was not hungry. Mum made a rabbit stew and she was also not hungry. It looked like a bunny and it tasted like a bunny and we must have been hungry. If you take the tail and head off, it looks like a bunny and you can't tell that it's a cat.

At the time, it was a great fear for children to get sick for lack of food.

By the time we got home, the worst was over and the occupying forces had stopped the lootings and rapes, murders and beatings. Everything started to get more orderly and quieter. Some ugly things did still happen at some times but on the whole, it was getting better.

Funny things also became known. Most of the Russian soldiers, it was easy to tell, were naive farm boys. Many times, when new groups arrived, they would march to the corner house, past ours. That's where they would eat. They had potato sacks wrapped around their feet and very ragged clothes on. The very next day, they would wear brand new uniforms. As they marched past us, they would sing "Opotzia, Opotzia," which was one of the songs, something about the old homeland. I did know what it meant at the time.

On random nights, two or three would knock at the door, you would be wise to let them in and let them take whatever was fancied and they would leave just as quickly. Most of the items were alarm clocks or watches. This must have been so special to them. But they knew nothing of these things, on the way out of the house they started to fiddle with it and the alarm would go off, with a loud scream they would throw the clock far away and you could hear them run for dear life. These sorts of stories were told many times and it did happen many times. We mostly felt sorry for them.

The time I left Austria with my mother and sisters, was the year 1952. The Russian Army was still in my home town.

My dad left for Australia the year before on a work contract for two years with the Australian housing commission.

After the contract was finished, we were told that we could stay as long as we wanted to, as workers were badly needed. As you can see, we are still here.

I was 16 years old at the time. Several hundred workers came with my father with the same work contract. And that's how I met my husband, your father.

In the year 1979, it was the first time that we went back to Austria for a visit.

I must say, I was very homesick all these years. I honestly expected to go back home after the work contract had finished.

It was very strange, first of all, no soldiers. The houses and streets looked so different. Hardly anything was the way that I had known in my childhood. My grandparents on both sides had passed away. It was not nice, I felt like a stranger. I did not belong anymore.

We stayed there for nearly 4 months, my dad had a big family and we stayed with them most of the time. Everyone was still the way that he left them. His parents, three brothers, and two sisters, all the families welcomed us.

But as for me, I cried a lot. It was all so very sad for me.

We had to travel to Frankfurt by train to board our flight back.

We went through this beautiful country, but my heart was so heavy.

As we sat in the departure lounge, I looked up at movement at a high window that caught my eye.

It was the tail of the Qantas plane with the red kangaroo. This did give me such a jolt!

"I am going home!"

Home is where my children are, I was homesick for my family in Australia!

CHAPTER 21

Nelly Needs Help

Nelly was surprised how well she remembered her mother's every word. She made up her mind to tell her children, Gary and Kathy, as soon as suitable.

She spent the whole morning being a nurse in Tom's room. That part was easy, that's her love, nursing. Tom got shaved, washed, his bed linen changed, the whole room was cleaned and some fresh flowers in a vase. The sun was just right, not too warm and it gave the room a beautiful liveliness.

So, why was she still restless? The doctor said something that she pushed into the back of her mind. While she was still busy it was easy to forget. But now, it was the next thing that she had to do and face.

She made herself comfortable as if that would be possible at this very moment.

She held her Bible close to her chest and prayed for some time. She needed some revelation from her beloved Lord. She needed help badly.

There was never any problem with this kind of thing for her; she loved to help other people. Come to think of it, some of them had really been curly ones and it did not phase her one bit. She just let God minister to her, but this one is at her own door, which was not that easy. Marg was her dear friend and sister in the Lord as well. She was the only one that knew her dilemma. They both prayed for Tom and Bill constantly.

But there was something that she had to do with her conscience and her God. He would be the one, who would tell her exactly what was needed and stop her hurting heart.

"Call him a bit louder, there is no other reason than this," the doctor's words echoed in her ear.

That's when it was most obvious to her that she was not doing the right thing.

With other patients, the first thing to do is to call them back to consciousness with a little slap on the cheek, saying their name, so they can wake up.

She felt very ashamed that she did not do this.

She could not bring herself to say his name to his face.

It was just too hard.

This not talking business between them… this backfired on her big time.

She did not want to face him because of the last few months and he might feel the same way, but she did wonder how he really felt about the two of them.

Opening her Bible, she went to the very back of the book, to some personal notes. Removing a stack of paper, this always helped her before, when she needed to help other people. She would read all of them, to see if she would come across something important and helpful.

Her Lord would point out the words that would apply to her.

The notes read:

If you don't forgive, the tormentor has the upper hand.

Very true, she thought.

Don't block God's blessings because of unforgiven and bad memories.
Obedience to our God is a very important thing to do.

Disappointments give you the feeling of being robbed.
Give it all to Jesus.
Blessings are renewed every day.
If you hang on to past hurts, the first thing they do, is rob you of your daily blessings and peace.
They are not worth hanging on to; they are cheating you out of your real life.
God knows all the good things that are in store for you, if you let go of all the old and also new hang-ups

Or, you tie God's hands, he is waiting for you to free Him and let Him do what He so desperately wants to do for you.

Let your God turn your scars into stars; for Him and His Glory.

Jesus had His scars, they are so deep, that it killed Him.

We must remember this and never forget: His love for us made those scars.
He found us worth it, to have these scars. That's how great His love is for you and me.
So, if your scars bother you, bug you, or even make you angry, no question about it, they hurt badly, remember one more thing, your scars would not be, if you did not love that person deeply enough and cause you so much pain, besides, only a very sensitive person would notice that you're hurting from whatever had just been said or done.

Most offenders do not even know of your pain, blinded to other people's feelings, their minds are too busy with whatever.
To hurt someone on purpose is an entirely different matter again!

We have and always will have days in which we are more sensitive than other days.

I find that if I am really "Prayed up" that nothing can get near me, that's when our Lord is fresh on my mind and I can feel His hedge around me. I feel safe from the darts that the enemy thrusts at me through other people. The enemy always looks for the slightest openings, no matter who they come through. The enemy's work is to hurt, maim, and kill.

The scriptures tell us:

When you've done all and everything you know to do, just keep standing firm.

Then it's the Lord's turn to work on our behalf. But, He is the one to say how and when, which is so hard for us to accept.

We want it now. Only, if, you let go of everything, is our Lord free to work on our behalf.

But He is still the one who says, when!

The favor of my God is upon me.

And He keeps my enemy from triumphing over me.

Pray for the Lord's favor.

Don't tie the Lord's hands, let Him do His thing.

Besides, He is the only one that knows exactly, what is needed in your life.

The apostle Paul must have made some strong effort about something for writing, "I must strain towards the mark."

A strong effort is often needed for certain obstacles

Everyone has many of those.

I refused to be trapped in the past; I will not let the past destroy my future.

Be willing to forgive yourself as well as others.

Give it all to Jesus and you will end up with the good for your bad and sad past.

Job. It's what you do, if you don't know why! God never told Job why all this misfortune had happened to him. Job just trusted God. As we read the whole story, trusting God no matter how long. Job had nothing at all left that was any good in his life. He never blamed God for it; he knew that the very last bit of life still in him also belonged to God. Job was blessed for his faithfulness with more than he had before. God wants us to understand this.

You and I are born of God. We are to be overcomers.

If it were not so, why should we need to be overcomers... If nothing was to overcome?

But now that we have lots of obstacles to fight, we are told how to stand and just do the very thing that we do not want to do.
So, don't ask why and do the standing firm, having faith in our Lord.

We do not walk by sight, but by faith, which is spiritual food for the soul.
Slowly we change, slowly we grow, slowly we become more Christlike, and slowly we will shine.

Walking by sight will not give us the things that walking by faith can give us.

Nelly put the papers down, thoughtfully she considered.

One thing was clear to her, no matter what happened, it was wrong.
"I have to swallow my pride, forgive and forget for my own sake. So no fault is on me.
But how do I do this?"

With a big sigh, she leaned back in her chair.
"Please Lord, show me what to do, I repent of my stubborn pride. I just want to make things right. But I don't know how."

Her thoughts went back to Tom's sins. If it didn't hurt so much it would be forgivable. Lots of men are guilty of such things, so why not forgive this one slip up?
Both went into a huff at one another. If she could get rid of hers? Would that make any difference?

"If I had no bad feelings about Tom, what would I do right now? I should go close to him, kiss him and call his name and wake him up!"

...Shock!

No, I can't do this!
Yes, you can. The voice came from her heart. Was this the right answer coming through?

She went close to the bed, hesitated, and almost changed her mind.

It's now or never, besides, he is asleep and would know nothing about it. But it would be good for her and a big step to take away some of her guilt.

She took a big breath, bent down, and put her hand on his cheek saying his name, kissing him on the lips.

Just as she lifted herself, he opened his eyes and smiled, saying "Love you Nell" and closed his eyes again.

Very startled, she stared at him. Guilt and confusion gripped her.

Feeling caught red-handed, she started to cry. "Now I feel worse than before!"

A soft knock at the back door brought her back to reality. She quickly refreshed her face and went to see, who this unwelcome knock belonged to.

It was Marg. "Thank goodness that it's you, I could not face anyone right now!"

Telling Marg about the reading of her notes and trying to get answers to her problems led to what just had happened the last few minutes.

Together they contemplated, Marg tried to reassure Nelly that it would have a good outcome no matter how things looked at the moment.

"What if a miracle brought Tom back to you?"

"Wouldn't that be something heavenly? He said he loved me the way he used to say it!"

"We prayed so much for this and now it's not so easy to handle. I suppose we will have to wait and see. But calling me Nell, the way he used to is so special to me."

Then she cried again, but this time with new hope.

Talking with Marg was the best thing she needed right then.

Very good timing.

CHAPTER 22

Disasters and Blessings

It was afternoon; Nelly was busy in the kitchen peeling potatoes at the sink.

Kathy came in and said, "I've finished my homework, now can I watch Telly?"

"Yes, but first set the table and tell your brother to feed the dog."

Kathy had a handful of cutlery in her hand and turning to the table, when Buddy burst into a frenzied bark, so loud that both of them rushed to the door.

At the very same time, there was this ear-piercing crash with the breaking of a window from the back yard sunroom, which was also Tom's sickroom. Both stood at the kitchen backdoor, facing the sunroom, that had the backyard door next to it. The boy ran towards them with a red face and yelled: "Mum, I am so sorry mum, it wasn't my fault, and mum I could not stop him."

All three of them yelling at the same time, trying to figure out what happened.

Kathy was holding the still very excited dog with one hand by his collar, who was still barking madly, fighting the fly screen door with the other.

"Explain yourself, young man!" Nelly was still holding a half-peeled potato, the peeler in the other, both hands dripping with water.

"I was playing with my ball when the big tomcat from next door jumped into the apricot tree. That's when Buddy went crazy; you know how he loves to get that cat. But he pushed me over and I tripped just when I kicked the ball and it got away from me. It all happened so fast, mum, I am so very sorry, but I could not help it, please mum, you have to believe me!"

"Ok, so why was the cat in our yard and in our tree?"

"Because the apricots are almost ripe and about 20 rainbow lorikeets were having a feast in the tree!

Mum, I am really sooo....Daaaddd?"

He lifted and pointed his hand past his mum and into the back of the room.

They all turned, looking straight into Tom's face, who sat, with both eyes wide open, tears streaming down his face.

Both children ran towards him, the dog was much faster, jumping right on top of the bed. The joy was overwhelming.

Nelly was speechless! She put the things at hand onto the side table, wiping her hands on her skirt. Then she saw the glass splinters all over the bed and blanket. She quickly went to the other side of the bed and started to remove the tubes from his arm. He looked straight at her as she busied herself with the bed, being careful not to disturb the splinters as she removed the blanket.

His eyes on her made her feel very nervous. "Please, don't let me wake up," he begged. She forced herself to look at him. "What do you mean? We waited for you to wake up for four days and you say you don't want to wake up!

You are awake now!"

Tom started to sob uncontrollably now, shaking his head.

Repeatedly saying, "I can't believe this, I can't believe this."

Cuddling the children and the dog, the noise was getting out of hand and the poor dog had to be put outside, with great resistance from Buddy.

Gary, enjoying his dad's attention said: "Dad you got a really big bump on your head, no wonder that you are a bit confused."

Tom could not settle down, crying and holding his kids, repeating words that made no sense to them.

Nelly went to the phone to call Marg. The medication Tom needed to calm him would have to come from her. Marg will have a clearer head than she did right now. Besides, she could not stop trembling.
Tom made no sense.

Marg came right over, assessing the situation and patting Nelly on the shoulders. "I think we could all use a strong cup of tea," sending her out of the room. Tom made no sense that was obvious, so she spoke very gently to him. He knew who she was, that was good. He wanted a mirror and that set him off again. Rubbing his chin, jaw, his hair, then examining the bandage on his head. Watching him, she did notice that he was very frightened about something.

Looking around the room, he spotted Nelly's Bible on the bedside table, he reached for it, "Oh, it's so clean!" He exclaimed.
Marg helped him pick it up and he took it in both arms and held it tight to his chest. Everyone was stunned.

Looking at Marg, he asked if Bill was coming over. This was awkward for Marg, now she was the one getting upset.
"Bill does not want to see me or anyone, he loves the bottle now."
"No, he doesn't, he is so upset with himself, that's why he was drinking."
"No, Tom, he is drinking every day, hardly knows his own name anymore."
"No no no, we prayed every day and we have been forgiven for our sins, you ask him, he will tell you."

This was getting worse, Marg was getting shaky. The big question now, what will we do to help him?

Just then, Nelly came in with a tray, teapot, cups, sugar, and milk, with Tom's favorite biscuits in a bowl. He was still staring at everyone, but when he saw the full tray, the tears started rolling again.

She handed him the tea with two biscuits on the saucer.

"Oh, Nelly, I can't believe that all this is happening, I tried so hard, prayed so much, this is a dream that I don't want to wake up from!"

"I need to see Bill, can someone send for him please?"

"Bill can hardly stand on his own two feet, let alone walk over here," Nelly said rather shocked.

"What's the bandage for, and why am I in the sunroom?" he looked straight at Nelly every time he spoke to her, it made her so uneasy.

She pulled herself together and started telling him of the day it all happened, every bit of it. Marg detected a good bit of anger in her voice, but no one else would know the bitter feelings connected with that fateful day.

When she told him about the day, Buddy jumped onto his bed and caused the needle in his hand to bleed and the bandage almost came off, she noticed that he quickly looked at his hand and nodded. She said that she thought that he almost woke up, but did not.

He nodded again, "That's when this nasty horsefly stung me."

"What's happening to me?"

"You almost woke up, so many times. We didn't know anymore what to think.

We prayed a lot for you; Pastor Robert and Helen came over and visited you.

Some other people as well. You talked a lot and we didn't know what you were talking about. You did talk with Bill and some other people."

"Nell, I don't want to go back, I want to stay here, please help me, I want to stay home, the way it is right now."

"You've been here all the time, Tom, you are scaring us all, the way you are talking. What do you want us to do?"

Marg went to the phone to talk to Dr. Kramer, advice was badly needed. He was very pleased with the news. He gave her the name of a sedative that would do just nicely.

Handing it to Tom, she told him how pleased the Dr. was and not to worry, in time all will be fine.

But Tom was afraid, that if he went back to sleep, he would end up again in that place that he so mysteriously escaped, as he put it.

Marg stepped in, "Well then, just relax and enjoy another cup of tea and talk to the kids, while Nelly makes a nice evening meal, you can do that, can't you Tom?"

She talked very softly to him, so he would not fight her about taking the tablets.

He seemed to do just that. He could not stop looking around the room, it was so very clean and his family was right there with him, he had missed them so much.

The evening meal was delicious to Tom. He thanked Nelly several times for such a beautiful meal. After the meal, Nelly sent Gary to Pastor Robert to come for a visit.

A little later, both arrived and happily greeted Tom. Marg was still there and all the news was told, as accurately as possible, waiting for Pastor Robert to help with the riddle, Tom was talking about.

After many questions, everyone decided to let Tom talk about what had happened to him.

The first thing he said, "How long does it take for a man like me, to grow my hair and beard this long?" He showed with his hands the length of his hair, the way it was in his other life. Everyone agreed that it would take at least several months.

"So, now that's my point. I was gone for that long. And I can give you names of all the people that were with me!"

He started telling of all those lives and goings-on.

Realizing that no one could testify on his behalf, he started to talk about the miraculous story with Nelly's Bible. He called it his lifesaver. Here was something that no one could deny.

Tom spoke with wisdom about spiritual things, the praying, the meeting, the joy of being forgiven. Then he turned to Nelly, and reaching both hands to her, he pulled her closer. "Please forgive me! I have no way of showing you how very sorry I am. I don't know and don't understand why all this had happened, but I will make everything up to you. I have learned so much about myself, all sorts of insights into my life. I have seen so much ugly stuff inside me. Our forgiving Lord has helped me so much with this. I have been given a second chance by God, so I humbly ask in front of all our friends… Will you give me a second chance also?"

With this, he started to sob.

Nelly and also all the others were speechless. This was too much for her. And it was quickly moving in a strange direction!

A knock at the back door startled them all. It was Mrs. Harris with a basket full of vegetables. Seeing Tom, she dropped the basket and headed straight for him with both arms wide open, it shocked them all that Tom put his arms around her and thanked her for being such a loving friend. He then told of the way the Harris farm looked, the last time that he saw it.

"Thank God that all is still well!" he said.

Mrs. Harris quickly realized that something unusual had happened to Tom, she was no stranger to spiritual encounters.

"Oh yes!" she declared, "Old nick was taking advantage of a weakness in you, but our Lord turned it into a good lesson for you."

"God always wins, we must thank our Lord. Pastor Robert, we have some thanking to do!" With this, she gave him a wink and Robert led them with a prayer that was very different from all the other times that they prayed before. After hearing all the new goings-on, nothing would be the same anymore.

Nelly would need some privacy for what Tom wanted, she needed time to think.

She was so glad about the interruption that Mrs. Harris provided. It was definitely the answer to her many prayers, only it was so very direct and final. That, she did not expect. Normally, God takes his time to answer prayers; this was not expected to be so blunt and direct altogether. So overwhelming.

Then Tom surprised them about the letter he read from Mrs. Harris and all the other letters. Of some that he read and some that he was about to read, and about the ones he wanted Nelly's permission for.

Nelly took the stack of letters out of her Bible cover and showed them all, that Tom was actually telling something that was not really possible.

But, Mrs. Harris nodded and smiled.

Now, she understood why she had to drop her sewing and take some vegetables to Nelly's house.

It always proved right, to obey the Lord's promptings.

As she made her way back to the farm, Fritz was waiting at the gate, he knew that something was going on by the way his wife took off, telling him all about it and both thanking the Lord for letting them be part of a need that they could help with.

Praying for people had great rewards and blessings all around.

The story about our devastated beloved farm was amusing and scary at the same time. "We must not take anything for granted." Both agreed.

CHAPTER 23

Home at Last

After all the visitors left, Tom got up, with the children's help.

Leading him to the bathroom was so much fun to them, because Tom was not steady on his feet. He longed for a shower but was very unsure of himself. "Please take your time and be careful," Nelly suggested.

After some walks around the house, all went well again. Even Buddy was allowed back into the house and he took full advantage of his regained freedom.

It was a very late night for the children, but a happy one.

Nelly did not know how to take it all, she felt rather uneasy.

Being alone with him and not knowing what to do next. She needed time to digest all the new developments.

She busily moved around the house, nervously waiting for him to make the first move.

Suddenly he grabbed her hand and a shiver went through her. He made her face him. "Honey, this is very hard for both of us, I know how much I must have hurt you and disappointed you. I need to show you how much has changed in my life. But we both need time to do this slowly because I have to do this right and not fail you again. I need to get to know myself and my situation is rather odd, don't you think?"

Now he held both hands.

"I really do love you, please give me a few days, I need to get to know myself first. I prayed so hard to get my life back and this time it's not only back, but so much more than it was before. I will stay in the sunroom for a bit longer and we will take it a day at a time. God willing, I will do what is right, with the Lord's guidance, we will have a very good life. Will you agree with this?"

He faced her with a pleading look and she started to melt in her heart, letting him know with a nod that this was a very good thing to do. He gave her a little kiss on her cheek and went back out into the sunroom.

She went to the bedroom, bewildered, and realized how very tired she was. But sleep would not come, she relived every moment of that whole day about one hundred times. How can anyone make any sense out of all this? Sleep was sweet this time, at last.

The next morning, Tom was already up and having breakfast with the children, even Buddy was munching on a piece of toast.
This was something new.
Happy faces so early in the morning.

The phone rang, Marg telling Nelly that it was a very quiet and slow day and she would ring, if she needed some help. That was good news for her; she could relax and have a slow day herself.

CHAPTER 24

A New Beginning

When the children left for school, it was very quiet in the house for some time.

Then the conversation started with the notes that fascinated Tom so very much.

"How did you get onto this book about the Armor of God? It's perfectly superb. It was the last thing that I read and it gave me such a lift, that I could read something with so many answers that I was struggling with."

The Bible was on the table and he took out the notes that he was talking about.

Now, Nelly was getting excited, her favorite subject was to talk about new discoveries. She got up and went to get the book, handing it to him, she found herself so happy to do so.

"Well, there is a little story to this, one day I got a prompting from the Lord to study the spiritual warfare in Ephesians chapter 6. I did not really feel like doing that. I told the Lord that this would be so boring. I forgot all about it for some time. Then one morning, I was watching a TV Program at 5.30 am. Rick Renner was being interviewed by Pastor Robson and he talked about exactly the same thing, that it would be boring to study Ephesians 6. I could not believe my ears.

He showed the book and all the things that he discovered. It really got me hooked, so I ordered it and I'm so glad that I did. But now I am waiting for the other one, a book called "A Light in Darkness" it has a photo of the apostle John's grave and other pictures like the cave of The Isle of Patmos. Things like that. I am looking forward to that one arriving, it should be here soon."

She looked at him and said, "Do you know how much it means to me to talk with you about things that excite me?"

He looked at her and reached for the book with, "Well, let's get excited together," a big smile and a hopeful expression on his face gave her many answers.

This would be a seriously good time to get to know each other in a brand new way. For the first day together, this was a very good start.

They went through all the letters that he had read. He wanted to know where they came from and how long she had been saving them.

There was so much exciting stuff to talk about, both forgot that the day was almost over and school was out. The noise of family life took over. Tom loved it.

Asking about school and subjects, likes and dislikes, friends and sports.

He thought to himself, what a wonderful family and life he had.

How could he had missed this and gotten things so wrong?

His life was not really a life at all before, what a wakeup call it took to realize his big mistake, it had taken a mountain size nightmare to see it.

For one split second, it crossed his mind he would once again wake up to this bearded, longhaired man looking at him in the mirror. With a shudder, he stopped himself and concentrated on the noisy house at hand.

The next day, it was obvious to both of them, they had a lot to talk about. Being keen to show all the other writings that she had saved for so long. She brought the folder to the table with so many special things that she treasured.

She proudly handed him a sheet of paper, "See this one? It's about the Great Southland of the Holy Spirit. It's dated the 14 May 1606, so it's rather old.

Can't remember who gave it to me. I have had it for many years, but I picked it up and read it again, I was really looking for something else at the time, as I read it, to my shock it was exactly the 14 May, but it was the year 2011.

It made me feel really odd and excited at the same time!"

Tom was eager to read it as well. He also found it an exciting treasure. Both went through all the other papers. He was going to read them all. Time passed and Nelly made some sandwiches and a drink for lunch, almost forgetting that it had only been one day in which Tom came back to her with so much beautiful life in him.

After the food, Tom remembered Bill, "As soon as I am a bit stronger, and my head stops thumping, I need to find Bill. I have to help him. I understand his dilemma, I think, from what he told me. He badly needs a friend. Don't know exactly what I will tell him. Will you be with me and pray for him? Before I go and see him?"

Another surprise for Nelly, "Of course, I will. Let's get Marg in on this too. Marg and I have been praying for a long time for both you and Bill. She would be so pleased if you could see Bill, he looks so sick; we think that he is not eating. This cursed alcohol has ruined his whole life."

Marg was on her way straight after work.

So it was settled. New hope was on the way for all of them. Marg was so very grateful, "We need another miracle; Tom has come back to us, better than ever! Bill will too, I just know it!"

Her tears flowed and her big smile showed that she would want nothing better.

Then Tom told them of all the other people that he had talked to and Nelly and Marg made notes of the names. Especially the two young brothers. He would visit them soon, and they, being of age now, would help them decide for themselves on what they would want to do. Prayerfully, Tom would softly talk to them and explain the options.

But Bill was on his heart, it would have to be soon. Both helped each other in that other world. They were very attached to one another.

Praying together and achieving so much, it would surely be a blessing for the real thing now.

But the Lord would have to help him with the right words, concerning an alcoholic.

He went to rest on his bed and think.

School would be out soon and a bit of quiet would be just nice right now. So much has changed in his life, so many good things and he was so very grateful.

Before he dozed off, he decided to ask Nelly to pray with him tonight and give thanks for this wonderful life and beautiful family.

CHAPTER 25

Life is Good

The days went by with a lot of joy. Tom was ready to visit Bill. A lot of prayer and good intentions went into this visit.

First, he had to find out where Bill live, and when he would be home. So far, he was told that Bill lost his job and moved into a little shack next to the railway station. This did not sound good. But Tom was keen, no matter how Bill would react to him. He loved him like a dear brother.

The shack looked very shabby, Tom knocked on the door, no noise came from inside. Tom stood for some time and then knocked much louder. After some time, Tom was about to knock again, when Bill's voice came through the door.

"Go away, leave me alone!"

Tom answered, "Bill, it's me, Tom; I really need to talk to you!"

"I told you to go away, I don't want to see you!"

Tom replied, "I did expect this, I think, and I told you, that I want to talk to you, and I am not going away till you do!"

After what seemed a long time, Tom knocked again, but, no reply at all. Sad and disappointed, Tom went home.

He did this every day for two weeks with exactly the same results.

"Next time I will stay and sit at his door, till he comes out. He will have to run out of drink or something."

He told Nelly.

They researched a lot of information, to see what they were up against.

So far, it was up to Bill, to give up the drink... just stop. No one else can do that for him. He had to want to give it up.

That sounded so very hopeless, but it was the naked truth.

"We will have to convince him to give it away, with the Lord's help and our persistence, we should be able to do it. But it will be a hard and long road, no matter what, we have to do it. It was very disappointing to them all, especially Marg, but both Nelly and Tom promised Marg that they will never give up. The church was also right with them.

Life itself was good at Tom's House. His office at the back of the house was running like clockwork again. Even better than before. Tom enjoyed his work that much more and his workload increased and the benefits showed also.

Tom's visit to the young brothers was very welcomed and the mother was very grateful.

Many other people came back to church; the story of Tom's nightmare was getting around.

Some of it anyway.

Then Tom ran into Sam, so surprised, because Sam looked so much younger than when he saw him last and he was so very polite, wishing him a speedy recovery.

At last, Tom faced Bill for the first time, his persistence paid off.

The conversation was not a good one, but it was the first step.

Tom pointed out to Bill that he would pursue him, till Bill would listen, and help him out of this addiction and get his life back.

Bill did not agree at all but knew that Tom would not give up till Bill gave in.

It was a very long battle.

Three months later, with many setbacks, many confrontations, and also tears from Bill, self-hate started to emerge.

Tom wanted so very much to share the nightmare that he lived with Bill, but Bill would never listen. But it did feel like that it would be soon.

But soon was a long way off.

Patience and a lot of prayers, together with strong friendship and commitment all paid off in the end.

At times it was hard, and it looked hopeless.

Now, Bill is on the mend and he and Marg are planning a wedding. Life is good again for all of them.

Yes, Tom thought, life is good.

THE END

ABOUT THE AUTHOR

Elfreda was born and raised in Austria, then, when she was 16, moved to Australia.

This is where she met her husband of 60 years, Otto.

They had four sons, who are now grown with their own families, with seven grandchildren and four great-grandchildren.

She loves her family and loves cooking. She has even written a cookbook for them.

She also loves gardening, reading, watching movies (especially scary ones!)

But most of all, Elfreda loves her God… And is totally dedicated to Him.

We hope you enjoyed reading her very first novel!

In my Grandmothers Garden

Illustration by Bronte Boyd

My friend Jesus talks with me

Illustration by Bronte Boyd